A Quiver in the Purlieu

A Quiver in the Purlieu

Amit Verma

Lake Dallas, Texas

Requests for permission to reprint material from this work should be sent to:

Permissions
Madville Publishing
P.O. Box 358
Lake Dallas, TX 75065

Cover Design: Jacqueline Davis
Cover Art: by Sergey Nivens and solarseven, and licensed through Shutterstock.

ISBN: 9781948692687 paperback, 9781948692694 ebook
Library of Congress Control Number: 2021938181

To my family

Prologue

Dear Orphia,

Forgive me, but I write to you in a time of extreme distress. I could have talked to you over the phone too, or even met you in person, and attempted to explain what you might consider my outlandish behavior. However, hopefully as you might shortly understand, there are reasons why I want to put everything down in writing. You are the only person in this world who can give me a sympathetic shoulder and help me out of this turmoil. Let me start from the beginning. This was two months ago when you came all the way to meet me. You see, putting this in a more or less chronological order will help me give it a touch of clarity, and (may I add for my sake) intelligibility (you are indubitably the smartest person I know). Thinking back to your visit, I must mention, as I did on numerous occasions, how much I enjoyed every moment. And why not! I am, after all, smitten by you. It was a gala time all around. If you remember, many a time during that period, you made fun of my habit of forming rules for everything and trying to stick to them. Yes, I have a clear reminiscence of a broad smile that would break across your beautiful, angelic face, whenever you would remark upon this habit, and warn me of troubles I may face as a consequence.

Please understand that I hold no malice towards you. I just cannot. I am too indebted to your love and friendship to harbor negative feelings. This letter is in no way intended to admonish you. This letter is for an entirely different reason. I must admit your perspicacious remarks proved to be prescient, perhaps even beyond your imagination. Without giving the impression of borrowing this from some tome, I realized how my rules have always lit the path in this otherwise uncertain journey called life, while your love has always given me the strength to undertake that journey. So, you see, I am supported by these two pillars, and when one pillar makes fun of the other, life can become perturbed.

After you were gone, and as I made up for the time spent with you away from work, I found myself in a situation I'd rather not bother you with, but it was somewhat related to your remarks. Please, I beg you again not to misunderstand me. I never found your words harsh. On the contrary, you helped me see this habit of mine in a new light when I most needed to. For the first time, I discovered that I am indeed a man of rules. I need to have rules for each and every situation, and I must stick to them. My rules may neither be entirely moral nor practical, but at least they help me avoid the daily confusions I simply cannot tolerate. Do you remember one evening when we were recollecting old times after dinner? At one point I asked whether you would prefer tea or coffee, to which you replied coffee. When I asked why, you said you just felt like it. Your answer and this incident, although wholly insignificant for most, including you, left a deep impact on me. This disposition of yours to rely on your feelings and instincts to reach decisions is what is so admirable about you. I am just incapable of being that way. You see, I have a very specific rule regarding this particular issue: I have tea only at one specific time of the day, and coffee at another. Of course, I am flexible about the exact time. I understand that a little flexibility is acceptable.

The more I thought about all this, the more nonplussed I became. I was astonished to find I had many more rules than I could ever count. Over the course of my life, I discovered, I have developed rules for every situation and scenario I have faced. How can I hope to keep track of all this? What if I face a situation I faced ten years back and do not remember how I tackled it then? I would be left helpless once more, trying to reinvent the wheel, wasting valuable time and effort unnecessarily. Worst case, it would be complete pandemonium! Forgive me, I exaggerate. Slightly.

This line of thought, and a few other matters too, forced me to do something dramatic. About two weeks after your visit, I reached the conclusion that I had to write everything down. Yes, each and every thing. I bought a thick notebook for myself, divided the pages according to broad headings, and started writing. I put down rules for what I am supposed to do in the mornings, evenings, and nights. I put down rules for what I am supposed to do at my workplace and at home. I set down rules for how I am supposed to treat my family and acquaintances. Believe me, it was an arduous task.

Into my second week of this attack of graphomania, I discovered that every morning my notebook was not the same as I had left it the previous night. It would be slightly displaced from its position. Furthermore, it started to feel slightly furry or woolly to the touch. Yes, to best describe it, hirsute. How odd! In the beginning, this bothered me little, for the changes, while discernable for the dispassionate, were barely so for the one burning with my single-minded determination. Soon, these minor physical changes accrued to something clearly noticeable. I further found the displacements and the furriness becoming markedly more distinct as I kept up my writing. But it was also around this time that the pressure at my workplace increased, and I had to set my notebook aside.

Two weeks later, when things returned to normal at work, I took the remaining vacation I had to finish the composition I had so dedicatedly started. I worked with a fervor that, at times, surprised even me. The task at hand was not easy. Not only did I have to write down all the rules, I also had to number them according to their importance. Many were interlinked and had to be correctly placed in the book. Many—and this was the most taxing of the tasks—many new entries had to be accounted for as they overwhelmed my fervent mind, running wild as it was with so many scenarios.

As the work progressed, I would increasingly find my notebook far from where I had last placed it, and with more and more visible hair. This continued until the time I decided to tackle the problem firmly. Each night, before I went to bed, I made it a rule to place a heavy paperweight on the notebook. This ensured I would find it in its proper place the next morning. As for the strange hair growth, I was at a complete loss. The hair was not long. It was a soft, velvety, and yet dense growth. The fur had the same walnut brown color as the notebook. Once I imagined it to be a mink-like fur, and perhaps without my consciously knowing it, I had laid my hands on a book with a cover made from the skin of a dead animal. This sickened me somewhat because you know how abhorrent I find cruelty to living beings: animals, birds, fishes, all of them. But then I thought I was just being stupid and paranoid. I thought that if you (yes, I thought of you), or anyone, looked at the notebook, you might be tempted to reason that the manufacturer had done a most exquisite job with the cover. However, as you will soon discover, as I also did later, I was not being paranoid. At that time, though, I was a man too possessed with my work to bother with all this.

Soon my little book of rules was approaching completion, and I was in for another unpleasant shock. I discovered that almost as soon as I would write a new rule, I would forget it. The only rule I could remember was to open the notebook first thing in the morning. I became completely helpless without it. It became an accretion to my body, and I had to carry it everywhere and continually refer to it. Looking back, I remember one incident that stands out. In a playful moment, I picked up a pair of scissors and cut a small piece of the book's cover, just so I could examine it more closely. Almost instantly, I remembered a few important entries I had made. Sadly, this obvious connection failed to register within me at that time. The book, as I found out, was growing by accumulating and hoarding the rules my mind was generating.

The final entry I made was four days ago. Oh, how clearly I remember it! The greatest day of my life! From that day on, I could move to the next stage of my mission. But even if my *undertaking was to be a failure, I would still have the book with me. From this point on, all I would need to do was look to the book for tackling any task, no matter how big or small. Euphoria? Yes, tremendous—but extremely short lived. All of a sudden, in front of my very own eyes, the fur opened up. I saw it all, and I will remember this forever. To my utter and sheer astonishment, it wasn't hair, but small wings. That book had developed wings! Those wings flapped a few times, and before I could react, off the book flew, out the window. I ran out the front door, trying to catch it. It flew past buildings and trees. What can I say? With total disregard for myself and everything around, I chased after it like a madman. However, as soon as this flying creature (for it could no longer be called a book), reached the river, its wings gave up. It seemed as if it had lost its strength. This creature of a book appeared to make a final attempt at fluttering its wings before plummeting towards the river. Dumbstruck and completely helpless, I saw it sink, slowly, lost from me.*

Orphia, for four days now, I have been living a wretched life. I hope you can understand my predicament. I am compelled to complete the book and so I'll have to gather my strength to restart. There may be no escaping this truth. Meanwhile, in all that I do, I now must feel my way around. Yes, feel. The new steps I take in this otherwise old arena are unbearably painful. If I do not feel lost, I am almost entirely helpless. This episode has taken quite a toll on me. But in the face of this extreme quandary, I request you, my love and my friend, to not consider this letter a desperate plea for help. It is on the contrary a first step, a feeble one, but a first step, nonetheless, towards my immense undertaking after an unfortunate hiatus. My instincts tell me the book is still there in the river, and perhaps I should refocus my efforts towards retrieving it. However, something about you and your unwavering trust in your instincts has come to the fore in my thoughts. I request you, Orphia, I implore you, when you receive this letter, please reach out to me. I am deeply interested in finding out from you the rules one must follow when using one's instincts in tackling any situation.

Chapter One

....

the universe expands to discover the reasons for its existence

In the end, I had no choice. The dreams were too vivid, too compelling, to ignore. It was there. It had to be. There was no other possibility. So, here I am, ready to dive into the river. Into that very spot. The water is dirty and polluted. I do not wish to die from a strange cauldron of afflictions one reads about in medical texts. But I still must do it. Fortunately, the river is quite shallow this time of the year, and I think I can mostly wade through it. The thick rubber boots should be able to protect me from any creepy creatures swimming in these murky waters.

This is the spot! The very spot. I know it. Even the water is of lighter color here. The glow. I see the glow! I'll get all dirty and wet if I take the plunge. I really do not want to take another shower. Really. At least no one is around this early in the morning. "What will they think," she would say all the time. No. It was, "What do you think they'll be thinking?" Yes. That's what she would say.

Well, here goes all or nothing!

One more day. I am tired. The same schedule in the morning. Waking up, getting ready, and reaching the office.

Why did I wake up at 5:00 today? The coffee should hit me soon.

Well, the work is alright. And I enjoy the company of the friends I have made at work and outside. Life could be much better, but this is not too bad. At least my evenings are much better.

Ooh, the trash bin has not been cleared. He doesn't seem to be taking an interest in the work around this complex anymore. And those cats from that house are very annoying.

It's already Friday. I should talk to Anita and see if she wants to join me this evening. Maybe not. Will it give the wrong impression? I don't want to complicate things more than they already are. I like it this way—simple.

Why doesn't the key go in? There, the door's locked. Now where did I park my car?

Cute child. Beautiful eyes.

I hate those dogs and their owners! What's with not keeping dogs on leashes? I am not obligated to like their dogs the way they do.

There's the car! I think I'll have to take it to the mechanic soon for an oil change. I wish my life was not so disorganized. Just cannot find time to do these important things. That electricity bill! Well, now I won't go back for it. Serves me right for not creating an online payment account.

And that phone bill, too! Don't forget to pay it today. Very important. I hope they don't disconnect my service. What will life be without a phone? I wonder what life was like before the phone. Jay's phone was disconnected a few days back. What a man! He can never get things done on time. It's not like he's doing something big and important in life. I am beginning to dislike him. Sort of pesters you and can be a real pain.

Life back then was really something. Simple, uncomplicated, unburdened. I wish those days could come back.

What's wrong with this car now? Good, finally it starts. This driveway is quite dangerous. I should try to make sure to park on the other side from now on. The road does not seem to be too crowded today. It's good to be this lucky.

Hey, what's with that guy? Doesn't he know how to drive?

Oh, no. That's a pretty lady behind the wheel. Oh, thank God. Braked just in time. Be careful when you drive and concentrate on the road. No need for that horn, no need for that horn. The radio. There. No, not this. News.

I wonder what happened to those keys I left on the table? I hope they're still there. I hate that fellow, *SB*. Always tries to bully me. Just my luck to find such a colleague. I hope his plane crashes.

No, I hope not.

Just cannot stand the sight of him.

If you are not thick-skinned, you will not be able to survive. Will not. No.

It actually depends. You have to be sensitive enough to enjoy the finer things in life.

Yes. Really a balance is required. Well, just do whatever you want and let the world go to hell.

Well, no. You have to bother about certain things. No total escape.

That's a very pretty girl!

It'll be good if I don't talk to Anita today.

It all balances out. Life takes care of itself. All these small things don't make a difference.

What was I just thinking about?

What in the world does this guy want?! Can't he look where he is going? Like the accident that took place in college. I was lucky to have escaped unhurt. I wonder what really happened to those two guys. Speaking of college days, I must call up all my friends. Better do it today when I get back.

Life has become tough lately. I miss the good old days when I had nothing to do. I wish I could have realized the importance of those days and done more of nothing.

I better get down to getting my act together now. No more procrastination. I must complete those two projects today. No exceptions.

It's a little difficult to manage time out of the office. What the hell is with the acceleration? So much for buying a cheaper car. Cannot even show your face driving it around town. I need a good, expensive car. No... I don't need it. Who cares? I don't need to show how rich I am. I have no concerns for the world and if this world wastes time looking at the car I drive, then that's not my problem. It would not make an iota of difference to me if I were to drive a good car.

Oh, I need to focus on my work. I'll have to sit down as soon as I reach the office and make a detailed plan and schedule for the way I want to get things done for the next couple of weeks. I think the biggest problem I face today is time. What an irony! A person like me facing such a problem. When will I learn that these things are really insignificant?

Sometimes I feel I have become quite egocentric. Maybe always was. Perhaps a narcissist.

Oh, now this traffic light! Why doesn't it turn green? I hope I find a great parking spot today. Hey, is that a department store? Never noticed it before. I need to buy a shirt over the weekend. I think I will go in for the one I saw yesterday. A bit expensive, but what the hell. If I look good in it, I won't mind that extra expenditure.

Oh God! Did I forget to put a stamp on the letter I posted yesterday? What's happening? Very uncharacteristic of me. Well, if I did forget, I wonder if the post office will send it back. Not a very important letter anyway. I hope nothing serious happens. No point in thinking about it right now.

Another traffic light! What's going on? Just my luck.

There is something soothing about this road. Very peaceful and pleasing. Quite unlike today's afternoon meeting. When am I going to get rid of those futile meetings? I should bring up the photocopier problem. One good thing about these bi-monthly meetings is I can sleep peacefully in the back row.

What is this guy doing in those tattered clothes? It's difficult to stand the sight of poverty. So much poverty, hunger, greed in this world. I wonder when it's all going to come to an end. Maybe never. Yes, maybe never. What was the reason for creating this universe and earth and all those stars? Waste of time. God, if He exists, should have spent His time on something more meaningful.

This is what is confusing. Should I spend the remainder of my life helping people, or should I believe it is solely up to each individual to improve his or her own lot? Maybe, with so much negativity in this world, I should try my best to remain aloof. The policy of not helping those who appear to be in position to help themselves is the best one to follow.

What a car! Beautiful. But what's the point?

The point is to let money flow. The woman in that car helped someone emerge from and stay out of poverty.

Zen philosophy says not to wish for anything. Great teachings. I should try to inculcate it in my daily life. I will not be able to enjoy life as I am doing right now, but maybe it will help me discover my true self in the process.

There is something that makes you stand apart from most of the people you see around you. I have a strong feeling that I am different from most others. I can notice it. They all have limited vision, and the same old ambitions in life. It's not that I am being egocentric in my thoughts. It's a fact. And there is nothing wrong in being ordinary, as most people are. If everyone starts thinking deeply about matters and takes a holistic view, there'll be a big mess and nothing in this world will ever get done!

Limited perspective has its own advantages. After all, I enjoy the bar.

I hate that *SB*. He personifies all that is evil in this world. He thinks he can get away with exploiting his juniors. Well, he must first tackle me. Let him try to get those papers out of me.

Negativity. Avoid that negativity. Only positive thoughts. Think about something else. Like what you can do over the weekend.

Weekends were so much fun back in college. Actually, weekends did not matter back then. It was so much fun, all the time. Enjoyable company, gala time, carefree life. Where have all those carefree days gone?

Nah. I still have those days. And better. I have all that, and now I have money. I think I am in a better place in life in all respects than I was those many years ago in college.

Now where can I find a parking spot in this place? I should try getting here on time to make things simpler. In a way, getting here late is a way of protesting against the environment I face throughout the day.

A very childlike behavior. I thought I was more mature than this.

Well, I will leave this place soon enough. I can feel it strongly. Things will be different then. Maybe not. Maybe, as I have a strong feeling, human nature is the same everywhere. I will find the same kind of people.

That wouldn't be so bad, would it?

Life is an education. All this is part of life. You learn from one classroom and you employ the lesson in another. I am turning into a philosopher! This is just great. Next step, spiritualism.

Thank God, I found a good parking spot. Now the walk to the office and facing the day.

The best thing about living is the fact that you feel. Not only just see, or hear, or think, but the sum total of all those things, plus something else, something much deeper. I am deeply in love with life.

At least I am better off than that random dead guy sitting in the backseat. I wonder why he decided to sit there when he could have moved to the front passenger seat.

Anita. I do not want to see her tonight. What did I do to get myself trapped into this? Her company is becoming unbearable. I, in fact, do not need anyone. Now why is this bloody elevator taking such a long time?

Good, got in the elevator just in time. I did not have to say hello to any of those guys.

The more I think about human existence, the more I find

that everything is meaningless. Whatever I do or think has no impact on the way things actually are. I am not here to make a difference to this world. Those who can, can stand up and do whatever they want. I just need a little space for myself.

The one way to accomplish this desire for space is to not take responsibility for my own actions. If I do something that others feel is wrong, well, I do not care.

I hope I'll remember this evening to talk to that dead person and figure out what he's doing in my car. I don't want to spend an hour stuck in traffic going home with him staring at me and talking to me. It's creepy.

There, the door, and the start of another work-filled, chaotic day. My energy is already drained. I hate it. Absolutely.

Chapter Two

....

the universe expands to escape boredom

The great truths, the greatest truths, are perforce always an exercise in refutation. Small truths, on the other hand, demand promiscuity towards the ages and the eras. Sometimes they connect. But I need to work hard to remember the two important narratives. One has to do with Ad, the dead person in my car. His name is Ad, short for something I could not quite catch. In fact, I could not catch most of what he said. I filled in the gaps at my leisure, with some discretion and considerable profligacy. So, his narrative here should be taken with a grain of salt. I am very glad we communicated.

Ad told me he missed his father terribly. But from what I could understand, this may not have been completely true. It might be more accurate to say he held very dear memories of him. Ad's father had died when he was only a little boy, perhaps eight or nine or ten years old. He had a somewhat strained relationship with his stepfather, or so it seemed. There was perhaps tolerance, and even at times acceptance, and occasionally, an understanding of the need for respecting his mother's whims and demands. It did not help that his mother was mostly too busy to acknowledge his existence. I think his stepfather, in actuality, adored him. It was that he was, maybe, just not his real father. Maybe ... who knows? To Ad, his father had been the perfect dad, a hero. He was strong, loving, and caring. And kind. He used to say to Ad, "Son, always be kind to others, no matter what. Remember, God is watching all of us. One kind act always deserves another."

Thereafter, Ad proceeded to tell me a long, meaningless story of why he loved to travel, and how this was an escape, in reality, from his stepfather, and a metaphorical search for his father. It was also an escape from reality, if you ask me. Here is what he told me:

"You may think I am dead, but that's only true if you believe you are alive. I am as alive as any one or thing can be. I am born out of time, and I will merge with it, when, well, my time comes. I can sense you shaking your head. You are not duty bound to agree with me. Let me tell you a story. No, it's not long.

I did not die in the way you think death to be. I did not stop breathing. There was no heart failure, no ugly disease. I was growing older peacefully and blissfully. By the time I was in my early middle age, I had everything I could possibly need. I had a decent car, a decent house, a TV, a beautiful family, a career. I could've had more, of course, but I could've had a lot less, too. Every weekday, like clockwork, my family would wake up, get ready, enjoy a quick breakfast, and leave for work and school. I would return in the evenings shortly after my wife, and much later than my kids. We would have small talks. Then we would get busy with our small things, until dinner. Shortly after that, we would retire to our beds, only to wake up the next day for a repeat performance. Weekends would be different, but almost always follow a routine that varied little. This went on for several years at a stretch. Sure, there are people in this world whose lives are full of so-called adventures and thrills. They are roaming the jungles in Africa or South America, or risking their lives in war zones, or simply sailing on long cruises. But the only reason they can do something like this is because many, many like me lead a life like mine, helping to build and maintain society. Regular routine work may be called drudgery, and any other epithets you may prefer to utter. And we may be called meek, docile, submissive, compliant. But this is the bedrock of humanity. This is what makes everything else possible—even defiance, rebellion, or revolution. Society and culture appear to only glorify those who try to lord themselves over commoners, or escape from them to seek glory in something different, and look down upon the likes of us, perhaps even consider us inconsequential and worthy of disdain and domination. They may do well to remember this: we are the ones who are embarked upon *truly* long adventures, sacrificing ourselves every day, little by little, battling all the uncertainties and insecurities thrown at us, perhaps grudgingly or perhaps enthusiastically. Yes, this includes even the lowly garbage collector among us, if your pretentious self may consider this necessary work lowly. We toil to make living possible, and we do so to hand over this precious world to the next generation. There is real stress in saving for a child's education, for your house, and working hard to do your job, and oftentimes simply to keep your job. You may consider it a sacrifice, or you may consider it a timidity in imagination and ambition for other grander possibilities. It is neither. It is a real adventure, and, if you are lucky, it lasts for decades.

I had this epiphany one fine weekend morning when I was sowing vegetable seeds in my small garden. I suddenly realized my importance, and I realized the importance of my work. I realized how I was contributing to society in a significant way. It all made sense. I looked at my family through the window finishing up breakfast, and I realized the larger role they were playing, unbeknownst to them. I now had another purpose in life, in addition to the already large burden I was carrying. I had to escape the deep-seated feeling, planted in me by the media, the movies, the books, by most everyone, that my life was meaningless, and perhaps even unworthy of the smallest mention. I had to convince myself, and all others like me, that we are worthy of celebrating, without any conspicuous celebration required. We do not need to project a sense of insecurity, a sense of unworthiness, by over-projecting a sense of success, a sense of being different from the crowd. We are what is good about this world. We are what makes it revolve.

How long ago was this epiphany? Not very long. Very recent, really. Maybe only a couple of months ago, give or take a couple of weeks, or perhaps only a couple of years ago, give or take a few months, or perhaps only a couple of decades ago, give or take a few years. For me, time is no longer the same as it is for you. I remember working in my garden with my hands, while my mind was excitedly churning out plans and possibilities. I could connect with like-minded people online. Perhaps I could write articles. Or perhaps I could shun a few aspects of my life, and let it be known to anyone who would ask, so as to encourage the closest to me to change their behavior. Lead by example, if you may. Or perhaps I could do all of those. I could conceivably do all of these things, while balancing my family and work lives. There are people who claim they can do everything. They claim one can squeeze out unlimited efficiency from a person with just cosmetic changes to the lifestyle. Or to an attitude towards life. They claim one can be as productive as one wishes. Maybe they are right. Maybe it can be done. Or maybe they are all charlatans.

But first I must digress and tell you about Hans. Yes, him. Don't interrupt. Have patience! Listen. Hans was my friend in college. A very close friend, or at least I had assumed so. We shared a room. I still remember the room. It wasn't much. I would say twelve feet by twenty feet. It had two beds, two tables, two chairs, and … OK! I get your point. I'll spare you the details. Anyway, in such close confines, you are most likely to either strongly dislike each other or become very close. And we did so, in that order. He was the flamboyant, outgoing type, the one who would make friends easily. Everyone liked him. I was the introvert, the one who, well, you know, tried to keep to himself. We complemented each other very well. He would help me open up, and I would help to keep his wild side in check. We were always together. Movies, parties, weekdays, weekends, you name it.

Then one day, I believe it was the end of our third year and we were packing up to leave for summer, Hans approached me, and asked for a somewhat large sum of money. He said he had met some unforeseen expenses, but did not elaborate, despite my prodding. Hans was very irresponsible with money, to put it gently, and I was always prudent. I wasn't completely surprised with his request. What surprised me was that this request had not come sooner. In the back of my mind, I always knew this was bound to happen someday. Asking his family for money would raise uncomfortable questions or concerns. I was the safest, most dependable person to approach. After a quick trip to the bank, I gave him the amount he needed, and then we parted ways.

This was the last I saw of him, forever. No message. Nothing. He simply vanished from the world. Later that summer his family contacted me. They said he had gone off one day and never returned. They approached the police, conducted a massive search, and even offered a large reward. I helped as much as I could. But there was no trace of him.

College was not the same when I returned. Fortunately, it was only for one year, and it passed quickly. I got a job in another, distant city, and soon Hans receded to a mostly inaccessible corner of my memories.

I heard he came back a few years later. But at that point, I did not feel the need to reach out and connect with him. People reminisce about their past, about the days gone by. They try to grasp at figments of memories with flailing hands, to save themselves from being hurled towards an uncertain future. I did not. I enjoyed my present, and I enjoyed waiting for the future. The past was gone. The past brought me to the present, and it is only appropriate for it to leave quickly after doing its job. I found it pointless to stick to the past. When I was alive, I always felt my present to be of interesting enough challenges, and my future to be of interesting enough potential, to keep me going. This is perhaps why I had a deep love for driving. I enjoyed driving. It gave me a sense of purpose. It reinforced my desire to take charge of the present and deliberately move towards the future. I loved driving alone, and I loved driving with my family. I loved long trips covering multiple states or driving through multiple countries whenever the opportunities presented themselves."

Ad then launched into a long, meaningless monologue of the different trips he had taken. Many of them alone and some of them with his family. He talked about driving across Europe, across Australia, across the southern parts of Africa. He had wanted to take his family on a trip to South America, but never got around to it. He died before that. At one point he abruptly transitioned into another monologue about the violin, of all things. He hated everything about violin, being around one, holding one, carrying one, playing one. He hated the "Brahms Violin Sonata Number 3." He hated his stepfather for trying to make him into an accomplished violinist by practicing that piece over and over. His stepfather's argument was that some famous scientist, probably Einstein, played violin, and so should he. At some point, all this devolved into a broader dislike for music. I think he enjoyed listening to music, the upbeat pop form of it. It was the more sophisticated forms he didn't like.

"I hated classical music. Absolutely. And I hated people who talked about it and wrote about it. Most of these people came across as pretentious, the showoffs, the ones who pretended their lives were anything but average. But I could see through them, see that they hated their lives. But if you ask me, there was absolutely no reason to hate themselves. I had come to the realization that normal, average, ordinary, typical, were anything but normal, average, ordinary, or typical. We, the ones who lead, or ever led, such lives are the true superheroes. The world is shaped by plenty of ordinary people doing ordinary work. And now I had donned the mantle of educating everyone of why we mattered more than anyone else, why books and movies should be about us. The last thing we should ever be doing is trying to escape our lives.

To mark this great alteration in my disposition, I began with taking a very overt principled stand towards my attitude and role as a social and family creature. I was going to fulfill my expectations, and I was going to be happy doing so. I started taking greater interest in my kids' schoolwork and homework. They hated this attention at the beginning. Couldn't stand it. They were used to me playing a background role, showing concern only when they produced their school reports. It wasn't as if I suddenly became an overbearing parent. No, that wasn't it. I just simply started taking an interest. If it wasn't easy for them, it was not easy for me either. But I had to do it. The next step was to start paying greater attention to my family finances, to take stock of the present, and be mindful of the future. I spent long hours with my wife, talking about our expectations, from each other and from the future. I spent even more time consolidating and investing. Investing and consolidating. I also started taking more interest in neighborhood issues and local politics. I actively campaigned for several candidates, going door-to-door spreading their messages. I also spent time, to the extent possible, following the news, reading, and following an exercise and fitness routine. It was all possible, I can tell you. As long as you have the desire, and you control your urge for the extremes, it's all possible. And no, there was no struggle with ennui. This was exciting. Each day would bring new challenges and new possibilities. Sure, things became routine from time to time. Everything done regularly and routinely loses its charms, even celebrations of the conspicuous or inconspicuous kinds. This is why you take occasional breaks, do something different, and then come back refreshed and rejuvenated.

This is why one exciting part of this new me was the plans for weekends and vacations. We were always making plans. Most of these never materialized, but many of them did. This is also when my love for driving was reinforced. Every few months, I would find myself on long road trips, by myself if my family or friends could not join me. But most of those trips were with my family, or at the very least with my wife or friends.

It was on one of those trips when my life changed again.

Trips, both long and short, were one of the perks I received for toiling in an otherwise mind-numbing, and sometimes, in rare moments of brooding, meaningless, job. If you ask me, so many jobs, and so many positions in the world today, are simply manufactured and unnecessary. It's as if society at large has taken on the responsibility of providing employment to as many humans as possible by creating irrelevant, extraneous positions. This has created a horde of otherwise highly educated people who are too afraid to exercise their intellect. This is all going to come to an end someday, maybe when the global population crashes.

One fine early spring day I found myself in Montreal, Canada, on one of these trips, attending a business meeting to finalize a contract. The trip was initially anticipated to last a few days. However, I was able to complete all my obligations within a few hours on the first morning. I now had those extra days available with nothing of terrible importance to address, and with a rental car paid for by the company at my disposal, I enjoyed a light lunch, talked to a few locals about areas of interest not too far from the city, made sure my cell phone was fully charged, and started driving. I drove and drove till there was nothing but thick canopies of forest surrounding me on all sides. The road would appear out of nowhere from the forest ahead and disappear back into the forest behind. Everything was perfect, and I found myself getting lost within in the depths of my wandering thoughts.

It was only a few hours into the drive when the weather became ominous. It started with a light breeze and soon the sky became dark with threatening clouds. The breeze quickly turned into a howling wind. Then a blizzard hit. Visibility turned to near-zero and I became seriously concerned for my safety. I was in an unknown country, in an unknown location, without enough clothing to protect me from the cold. My cell phone was not picking up any signal, and the fuel was running low. At one point I decided to pull over and try to outlast the storm. I had a parka in the backseat and a change of clothes in the trunk. If I bundled myself, I thought, I could perhaps weather the cold. I soon saw a glimpse of a side road. Without thinking further, I took this road and drove a small distance before pulling off to the side and turning off the engine. I pulled the parka over me, switched off my cell phone, said a small prayer and tried to go to sleep.

It was almost four in the morning when I woke up. My body ached from being confined. The blizzard had passed, and the sky was perfectly clear. It was still dark, with a blaze of stars overhead, and I could make out a long wooden fence. Straight ahead down the road, perhaps a half mile away, was what seemed to be a large farmhouse. It appeared that I had pulled over by the side of a sprawling ranch. With nothing else to do, I lowered my seat and went back to sleep. When I next woke up, the time read six-thirty. I could see clearly in the early morning gray, but the sun had not yet risen above the horizon. I stretched and looked around. The farmland was now completely visible. Its vastness stretched before me. It was mostly grassland, with fine thin grass, and a few heavy-set maple trees dotting the surface, giving the vista some character. There was no accumulation of snow or ice visible. This must have been one of those fast-moving storms that early spring weather throws in northern climes, like angry parting shots from a receding winter to an approaching, but still distant, summer. A few cows and goats were fully self-absorbed in munching on grass. One cow, though, had taken an interest in me. It gazed at me intently, its head jutting out over the wooden fence as it methodically chewed on grass. I do not know why, but that cow left a vivid impression in my mind with those wide big eyes and the curiosity exuding from them. I strongly believe it was trying to formulate the right words to say to me. Perhaps it was asking me to pass along the message that it did not see the point in being killed to satisfy someone's cravings, especially when so many plant options are available, flavorful, and far healthier."

No, I made up the last part. Ad never conjectured about the internal state of the cow. I, on the other hand, never miss the opportunity when I talk about animals. Ad described the drive over the gravel road to the farmhouse after he had stretched and rubbed the sleep from his eyes. He described the house as mansion, belonging to people who had time, taste, and money. The house and the farmland belonged to an aging couple who were polite and welcoming, at least on the surface. They took Ad in, allowing him the use of their bathroom, providing him with a towel for a hot shower, serving him breakfast, and spending considerable time talking about themselves, with occasional, curiosity-filled questions directed to him.

Ad said, "A couple of hours later, and I was ready to get back on the road and head back to Montreal. This was more adventure than I had bargained for. I was ready to call it quits and spend the next few days at the hotel and do a quiet exploration of the city. As I was stepping out the door, the man—I never got their names and I am sure they never got mine—put a hand on my shoulder and said, 'I've got something for you, something as a parting gift, something to remember us. Come with me.'

We walked outside and around the house to a bright red barn, with an adjoining big, brighter red garage. He led me into the barn through a side door and motioned for me to wait in a corner. He crisscrossed through piles of hay to the opposite wall and came back with a closed fist. He unclenched it to show me a single brownish seed.

'Here, this is for you. I felt you, of all people, would appreciate it,' he said.

'What is it?' I asked.

'It's a banyan tree seed. Take it with you and plant it in your yard.'

'Banyan tree? Why would you have a banyan tree seed so far north in Canada? Do banyan trees even grow here?' I asked.

He gave me a look not dissimilar to what that cow had given me, just more quizzical. He said, 'A banyan tree will grow wherever you want it to grow. It will grow at the equator, and it will grow at the poles. You just have to plant it, nurture it, and, I believe, not do anything too extreme to harm it. You seem to have the sensitivities to be able to grow it. Trust me, I've seen many, many more summers and winters than you. I've also grown a banyan tree. This seed comes from there.'

I asked him if he could show me his tree. He agreed gladly. We walked together through his vast field. We passed by cows, goats, and sheep, and three big dogs. The dogs were as friendly as the man and his wife. They rushed towards us with wildly wagging tails, sniffed me, and then followed behind. We eventually reached a far corner of his property where a small but thick canopy marked the boundary. The canopy consisted of a cluster of maple trees just starting to bud after the winter. It was within the canopy that I saw it. It was a thick, lush banyan tree, with long, thick, and uncountable tentacles reaching down to the ground over as wide an area as one can imagine, a truly magnificent tree. Did I mention it was lush green? Yes, it was. And consider that the weather was still cold and consider that this was Canada. No banyan tree should be growing here in the first place. We stood in silence for several minutes. All the while, he looked at the tree dotingly, and I with bewilderment. When he was done admiring it, he turned towards me. Thereafter we walked back, in silence again, to my car.

I was in my hotel room a few hours later. During the drive back, I had called the airline and rescheduled for the first available flight. Once home, I wasted little time. I took the seed to my yard, cleared a circular patch a couple of feet in diameter in its center, and planted the seed in a small hole.

Next morning, I placed a small garden wire netting around the seed to protect it. Next day, I sprinkled a small amount of high potency fertilizer. I watered it the next day. The following day I used a garden trowel to weed the area. I watered it again the next day. It was the next morning that I saw a small shoot had emerged from the ground. I finally slept peacefully at night.

Over the next few days, I saw the plant display incredible growth. I removed the netting and inserted a fertilizer stick near it. I then went on a ten-day summer vacation with my family. When we returned, we came back to a full-fledged banyan tree. It was not as big as they can get, and not as big as the one I saw in that farmland in Canada, but it was fairly big and growing. I could not feel prouder of myself! Here was a tree, where only a few weeks ago existed a small seed obtained from a most unlikely place.

I would visit the tree every morning, oftentimes with a cup of tea in my hand, and admire it from a short distance. I would have dreams about the tree too, you know. Those were good dreams. They were comforting dreams. They were relaxing dreams. I would wake up fully refreshed and charged whenever I had such dreams.

I cannot recollect the precise moment it began. I know it was a few months later. My family was gone for a couple of weeks, visiting relatives. I used their absence to spend as much time with the tree, and under the tree, as possible. At some point I noticed my hands would blend with the hanging roots of the tree whenever I touched them. It was subtle at first, but soon became very obvious. Whenever I held the tree, my hands would appear to meld with it. This was astounding and truly exhilarating. I started spending even more time with the tree. For hours at a stretch, it would be just the tree and me. I would watch with fascination as my hands would fuse with the tree when I touched it and emerge from the tree when I pulled them back. Fuse and emerge, fuse and emerge.

One beautiful morning, a day or so before my family

was to return from their trip, I stepped into my yard, rushed towards the banyan tree, gave it a big, tight hug, and completely amalgamated with it. I soon blossomed as a root from a low-hanging branch and dove towards and then into the ground. Underground, I spread my tentacles and planted myself firmly. Thereafter, I died from the world you know."

The story did not make sense to me. Here I am, hurtling through the dark depths of this cold, desolate, inhospitable, and hostile galaxy, clutching the thing that matters most to me and trying to get back to my life. I have nothing to do but reflect on the time gone by and hope for the time yet to come. I just wish he was more exegetic, if for nothing else than to have made this return journey more tolerable for me. Now I must deal with this itch until the world I know takes over and defines my thoughts and actions and time for me.

"It doesn't make sense," I told him when he had gone silent.

"Neither does the "Brahms Violin Sonata Number 3" to so many of us. But does it mean it's meaningless? Worthless? I am not here to make sense of everything for you. It makes sense to me. I've told you my story. And please do not tell me your story. I know it and am not interested."

"But why are you here? You say you are dead. And I know you are dead. You should be with the banyan tree."

"I am. I still am. I am still connected to it. But I had to materialize here. I am bringing important information for you. You need to see Hans."

"Hans? Your long-lost friend from your college days? The Hans I know? The same Hans?"

"Yes. He is at the dark end of the galaxy. But he should be easy to find. They always are. You need to see him."

"Why?"

"He has the book."

Chapter Three

the universe expands to fill the voids

I still remember the day clearly, even though I was just seven or eight at the time. Our village had a new visitor, and everyone was agog with a concealed, yet effusive, excitement. The newcomer was a *Swami*, a holy man. He was dressed in saffron and held a small trident in one hand. He was quite thin with a pale face. His face, though in stark incongruity with the rest of his demeanor, supported a thick black beard. After visiting the temple at the center of the village, the *Swami* made himself comfortable under the banyan tree right in front of the temple, and next to the biggest, deepest well within the surrounding few villages. He then stayed there for the next thirteen years.

That night it rained hard, allaying any fears of a possible drought. And, indeed, there was no drought for the next thirteen years.

In the beginning, elders and children alike were apprehensive about talking to him. I know for a fact, though, that most grown-ups felt a visit from a man of God was the best thing to have happened to this village as far back as they could remember. I used to hear my father and his friends talk late into the night about this serendipitous event. The village was at a good distance from even the nearest rail line, and was thus never within the radar of the outside world. The small size of the village too made it inconsequential to the outside world. Occasionally, and that means once in a few years, a handful of political workers would swarm in, riding in all kinds of vehicles, attempting to draw the attention of the villagers. But nothing of any significance happened here. Life was isolated from the major events happening elsewhere, and therefore tranquil as only an idyllic, rustic life can be. The population was not more than a few hundred and everyone knew almost everyone from the last three generations. The usual social hierarchies were observed only loosely when villagers congregated at social events, because everyone sooner or later needed everyone. Though, of course, important activities like marriages were conducted mindful of time-honored traditions and societal norms. The village center, which had the temple and a well, was also the most important place for the villagers. It was not unusual for people to gather there once every week or two. My house was on the eastern side of the village and was the biggest in the area. The village also had an elementary school with one teacher. I, like everyone, adults included, used to simply call the teacher *Sir*, and to this day I do not know his real name. My father once told me that *Sir* came to the village a few years before I was born as part of an outreach effort by a non-governmental organization. He fell in love with the place, and never left. In time, he earned much respect for his admirable character, and people came to trust him for educating their children. This is how the school formally began. So, four days a week, I would take a mile-and-a-half long walk to the other side of the village to attend school in the mornings, and then walk back home in the afternoons. On the way back, I would usually spend an hour or two near the temple playing with my friends. That is how I came to observe the new guest closely.

The *Swami* was the first to move in the direction of making acquaintances. This began with the temple priest and then slowly expanded to most everyone in the village. The miracle of the rain, his general solemn demeanor, and at times, a severe and deathly look on his face ensured that the

Swami commanded enormous reverence. He spoke little, but whenever he did, it was with a sense of gravity. People would approach him with their issues, and he would advise them in wise, terse sentences. Everyday, from one o'clock in the afternoon to four, come rain or sunshine, he would shut his eyes and meditate. Complete silence would descend during those three hours, broken only by chirping birds. Surprisingly, even the famished mongrels would stop barking. People would make sure to tiptoe around him. Mothers would hold their newborn babies closer, lest they start crying and disturb the trance of the *Swami*. Children would stop playing and move away to carry on with their activities elsewhere.

My friends and I found this a trifle bit annoying in the beginning. Like most young children, keeping silent while playing was not what came naturally, and we griped at being forced to look for a new play spot. That area around the temple was an important part of our lives, and no other place was ever going to be good enough.

Soon, however, I began to pay more attention to the *Swami*. It was bound to happen. My own curiosity notwithstanding, the talk all over the village about him by elders, and the fact I would see him almost every day, all contributed their part in my curiosity. What really broke the camel's back and brought us close was the day my father took me to seek his consul. That morning, I was pulled away complaining from the little game I was engrossed in by my mother, given a quick bath, put into nice clothes, hair oiled and combed, and dragged by my hand by my father. We stopped only after we had reached the *Swami's* abode. There he was, the *Swami*, sitting under the tree looking serene, with eyes half closed. He was listening intently to Prem, a small farmer, pouring his heart out over his desire to have a male child. His wife had given birth to their third daughter a day before. Everyone in the village, from small children to wise elders, had heard the news and felt sorry for him. But it was still captivating to hear him bare his emotions for the public at large. After he had dropped a tear or two, my father went up to him and put his hand on his shoulder. Prem stopped midway through a sentence, looked at my father, wiped his tears with his arms and gave the *Swami* a beseeching look. The silence caused the *Swami* to look up. In doing so his eyes met mine and rested there for more than a moment, before moving to Prem. The *Swami's* reply, which caught my fancy and caused no small amount of consternation for those present, was characteristically crisp and incisive.

"A life is too short to waste on insignificant and trivial issues. Go away! Go away and wait for your end with joy, for there is no problem!"

The *Swami* then closed his eyes. For a brief moment I felt he was trying to control his temper. But very soon he was calm again. As soon as that happened, people around began whispering in unison. Prem tried to speak again but was immediately unnerved into silence when the *Swami* opened his eyes and fixed a hard gaze upon him. Prem took the cue, and with a dejected look, turned around and walked back. As he did, people made way for him and then covered his tracks. As soon as he had left, my father walked up to the *Swami* and spoke in a low and respectful voice.

"*Swami*."

He said nothing and kept his eyes closed.

"*Swami*," my father said again, now with a degree of anxious uncertainty. He then placed both hands on my shoulders and brought me closer, as if he needed some support. The *Swami*, without opening his eyes, said, "Yes. What brings you here today?"

"*Swami*, this is my son." My father pushed me in front of himself. "I have come here because I need some advice regarding him."

"And you think my advice will be proper and correct?" he asked, eyes still shut.

"I have no doubt, *Swami*," my father replied with all the

respect he could muster for someone so important in the village, and he did a good job of it.

"Life is fickle. Be afraid and apprehensive of the future, and the past will devour you. Be rooted in the past and the future will overwhelm you. And yet, and yet," at this the *Swami* opened his eyes and rested them on me, "sadly there is no escaping the present." He then closed his eyes again.

None of us, least of me, could comprehend what this meant. But this proceeding was becoming more and more intriguing for me. My father, who then decided that a more direct approach would probably be better, said, "*Swami*, I need your advice on what I should do for the future of my only son. I have great hopes for him. Should I send him to the city for higher education, or should he stay here? I want him to live in the city for a few years and learn about the world. He can then come back and apply his knowledge here. I want him to know all there is to know, and to do all that I could never do. But, I am still a father, and a husband. My wife and I cannot bear the thought of sending our only son away from us. My wife especially. Her life revolves around him. I hope you understand my predicament. Please give me some advice."

On hearing this, the *Swami* frowned a little. Everyone around looked on without blinking, as if every approaching second was more fascinating than the previous captivating one.

"Ask yourself first," the *Swami* said. "Do you want my advice, or do you want me to shoulder some of the responsibility for your decision? However," the *Swami* again opened his eyes and looked at me, "I have often had the occasion to notice your son. He looks bright, so full of life and energy. The future should belong to him. As for me, I am soon going to die. My body will wither and ultimately unite with the earth. My soul will continue its onward journey. But life will go on. It will go on. And your child, like every child, represents that life."

The *Swami* then fell silent. During that time no one spoke. After about thirty seconds he continued.

"You should, I feel, invest every opportunity you get to broaden his horizon. Make him a better human being, someone you can be proud of. You should send him to the city for education. And now, the time for my meditation approaches."

As abruptly as he had ended the conversation, he moved his gaze from me to my father, then to everyone standing around, and then closed his eyes. We slowly started walking away. Turning around, I saw a few people dispersing, and a few sitting down cross legged and meditating with the *Swami*.

Over the next couple of weeks, and after lengthy discussions with *Sir*, and a few others in the village, it was decided that I would go to the city in the coming year for schooling. I was to stay with my maternal uncle who had moved to the city a few years back, and who had first put the idea of city schooling into my parents' heads. How did I feel about all this? It is difficult to say, now that decades have passed. Time clouds most emotions. I do somewhat remember being uncertain and apprehensive. But that cannot be correct, can it? Perhaps I am just projecting what I think I am supposed to feel about the past. In any case, there I was, a small child, away from home, in a big city. My uncle and aunt took good care of me. My cousins and I became very close.

I returned home once every few months. For the first few years those visits had all the markings of big festivities. There would always be a large group of people waiting at the railway station to receive me. In fact, the very first time I returned and stepped out of the train and onto the platform, a small prayer ceremony was held at the station, followed by a celebration that consisted of a dance by the local troupe and distribution of sweets! Following this was the procession of the long journey back to the village, with my family and me on a horse-and-buggy, surrounded by other horse-and-buggies. For two long days I was not allowed to leave the house. There was always someone waiting to see me, eager to hear my experiences of the city. When I finally found the time, I did what I had been dying to do ever since I left the village: I ran to the village center to meet the *Swami*. He was still there, still sitting serenely under the same tree, in the same posture, surrounded by the same small crowd. I went straight up to him and sat in front. He must have felt my presence and in time, opened his eyes and gazed upon me.

"You are back," he said with no expression.

"Yes, I am," I replied, beaming, in huge contrast to his demeanor.

"Tell me, what did you learn in the city?"

And for the next half an hour I told him everything. I think it was my innocent exuberance that caught his fancy, because this was the first time that the *Swami* was late for his meditation. When I was done talking, he had only this to say: "I am glad you are excited about this change in your life. Life is sometimes too short, and changes are not always for the good. Count yourself blessed. Anyway, you are too young to understand this. Go now, for I need to meditate."

He shut his eyes, and I left. My next meeting with the *Swami* was during my next trip home. This, too, soon became a ritual. Every time I came back to the village, I would visit him at least once. I would tell him about my experiences and life in the city, and he would reply in a few sentences, oftentimes pithy. As I grew older, though, his sermons to me took a turn for the melancholy. They would often focus on death, and almost always had a conviction about the wickedness of fate.

During this time, big changes around were taking place. Our village was now connected with a fairly wide asphalt road. There was also a talk of a railway line passing near the village. The fame of the *Swami* was also on the rise. People from distant villages started to pay him visits. At first, he was slightly bothered by this intrusion and what he felt was misplaced exaltation, but he soon came to terms with it. He once told me about this matter in one of the rare occasions when he entered into a two-way conversation. However, there was also something else unsettling him, which I could instinctively sense. He seemed to be growing paler and paler with every visit I paid him. It was as if he was waiting for something—a divine communication maybe—that wasn't happening.

Importantly, I was also getting older. I was passing from adolescent to manhood. I was becoming more and more driven, a person on the go, with a nascent ambition taking shape. The *Swami's* sayings on life and death were always playing on my mind, defining my thoughts and actions. He once said, "Remain without attachments and you will float over life, just like a flower floats on a river. Life is like a river, moving inexorably towards a waterfall and not the ocean. It only flows faster and faster. Just as a river gains speed to meet the inevitable fate head-on, over the falls, so too life picks up pace to culminate in the end. Do what you have to, achieve what you have to, for when your life starts moving rapidly, you will have no choice but to follow it, both in direction and speed."

When I was twenty, and in college, I came home for my regular visit during the summer. Everyone was now used to my being away—thirteen years is a long time—and so there was no longer any crowd to welcome me at the new railway station nearer to the village. There were also not nearly as many visitors at home. The day after I arrived, I decided to visit the *Swami*. His countenance during my previous visit had left me slightly concerned. He had grown thinner, and there was a whisper going around the village that he was approaching the end. However, as I never received any message to that effect from anyone, I had assumed the unmentionable had not happened.

The village center, like the village and the larger surroundings, had undergone a transformation over all these years. The temple had become bigger. A few more shops had opened around it. The banyan tree, under which the *Swami* lived, though, had remained the same. To my surprise I did not find him there. Not even a trace of his meager belongings. It was then that I feared the worst. For a moment, I felt angry at my parents for not informing me about his death. Slowly, and in daze, I made my way towards the temple gate, where I ran into an old friend. I asked him.

"I had come to meet *Swami*. But I see he's no longer here. When did he pass away?"

"Oh! He never passed away. He left," my friend replied. His voice had an unexpected tinge of excitement, in contrast to the grave topic at hand. He was clearly aching to let me in on a story.

"What?" I was perplexed. "When?"

"Two days ago!" he replied. "But, of course, you wouldn't know about it. You just came home yesterday. A very surprising thing happened. Two days ago, someone came to meet the *Swami*. It turned out it was his brother. A very unfortunate case indeed."

"Why? What happened?" I was finding it difficult to handle the suspense. After all, nothing less than the pivot of my life up until now was involved.

"Oh, very unfortunate. It was all the fault of the doctors. Never trust them."

"Tell me." I was now decidedly testy. Any further delay, and I feared I would shove him to the ground.

"Well, it seems that before the *Swami* became *Swami*, he was living in the city. One day he fell ill, and the doctors diagnosed him with an incurable form of leukemia. They didn't give him too long to live. He decided to renounce everything and lead the remainder of his life as a hermit. Escape everything and everyone. Completely. The crux though, and this is the crux, was that he never had cancer! Aren't you surprised?" my friend asked with a childlike glee, which was amplified by the big nose and small eyes on his pointed face.

"What do you mean he never had cancer?" I asked.

"This is what I mean, and this is what his brother told him. Seemingly the doctor had mixed up his diagnosis with someone else's!"

"Oh," I replied.

I walked pensively back home. The village had a drought that year, the first time in thirteen years.

When I was twenty-five, perhaps twenty-six, I joined a stamp collectors club. It was composed of a handful of dedicated philatelists, with a few other semi-regulars. We would meet on the first Tuesday of every month at the local library, and discuss all things having to do with stamps for a couple of hours. We would view, many times with envy, each other's collections and new additions. We would also talk about new releases, and how best to acquire them. Discussions would sometimes touch upon personal lives, but often drift towards the history of those stamps, and history, present state, and future potentials of the countries those stamps came from. There was never a dull moment because there was always something new to learn. And one had to come prepared for discussions, especially if one was to show, or show off, a collection. This was not always easy. Collections tended to be large, with some very rare stamps among them. In the age when the internet was not commonly available, and internet search engines were just coming into vogue, digging up information was always a challenge. Fortunately, our club was a repository of information. And what information we could not dig up in our hive-minds, we could try to locate at the library. At the cost of sounding immodest, I had an outstanding collection. It was certainly not the best among us. That accolade went to Charesh. The next best, in my opinion, went to Mauna. My collection was, I think, the third or fourth best. But it was still something I was proud of. In my collection was a triangular stamp from Chad, which none in the group had, and which was my favorite. If one day I forget everything about my collection, the one stamp I'll never forget will be that triangular stamp. But there were others I liked, too, not only because of their beauty, but also because of the history and information they carried with them. I had a few striking stamps with realistic drawings of animals from the country called Bophuthatswana, which ceased to exist in 1994. Like any human being, a country too is born, and can die. Once that happens, it may perish completely and dissolve into the graveyard of history. Or it may lie in wait, waiting for resurrection, to haunt the world. If there were any stamps I found that were traps for ghosts of the past, they were stamps with pictures of Stalin. They were eerily mesmerizing stamps. They had Stalin in different poses but with some similarities that went beyond just the well-trimmed walrus mustache. They showed him with gentle kind eyes with a faraway look over the horizon. Mauna interestingly had a stamp of Stalin from his youthful years. In it, he had a somewhat thinner mustache and was staring into the camera, as if he was watching you, as if he knew you, in your heart, were anti-Soviet, as if you had discovered the cover-up that was the Soviet Union. One almost never finds a similar stamp from any authoritarian regime. China doesn't have one. The tiny island of Taiwan, or the Republic of China, tries to make up for that deficit by gazing at China with a single eye across the channel. But it has rarely, if ever, done so through its stamps. Compared to its history, I find the stamps from Taiwan to be very anti-climactic. Perhaps this was done intentionally.

It was Orphia who, one day, as we were at our meeting showing off our collections, gave us a brief talk on the history of Bophuthatswana. She was not an avid philatelist but had dabbled in the hobby as a child. She was at the library during one of our meetings, searching for good mind-numbing chick lit, as she told us. She happened to pass us by, eavesdropped on our conversation, and thereafter forced herself into the group. She brought her collection the next meeting. The meeting after this she brought a friend along who flirted with Charesh. The two hit it off very strongly after our meeting, leaving Orphia and me to engage in small talk, with one eye on our watches and the other on the two of them. At the beginning, the small talk was just that, small. We complimented each other on our collections, talked about the weather and our vacation travel plans. However, we soon found that we had both attended the same college, just a couple of years apart. She had graduated with a degree in aerospace engineering and I with a degree in computer engineering. The biggest connection was that we both worked in industries with many commonalities and shared connections. Our nature of work was also very similar, which largely consisted of attending too many meetings, writing lots of reports, troubleshooting systems we were not involved in creating, and dealing with recalcitrant customers. It was a pleasant, semiprofessional conversation, and by its end, we exchanged our professional contacts, and agreed to be in touch, with the feeling that in an uncertain job market, we could be helpful to one another. It did not go beyond this for some time.

Orphia apologized to us all at the next meeting for the distractions her friend may have caused the previous meeting. Mauna gave her a slightly condescending look but spoke no further. Charesh kept quiet too. Orphia later told me that Charesh and her friend had gone out more than once over the last four weeks and planned to continue seeing each other. With her apology out of the way, it was my turn to start our meeting with my collection. I pulled out an assortment of stamps from Bophuthatswana I had separated out from my main collection from the country. This smaller number of stamps had, I felt, the most beautiful and vivid drawings of animals from the wild. I passed them around for everyone to view and admire. The one that caught Orphia's attention the most was of a bushpig. She raised it to the light to take a better view through its transparent polyethylene sleeve, used primarily for storing film negatives, which is how I stored all my stamps. After a careful gander, she commented on how gracefully and unrealistically the bushpig seemed to be trotting.

"Much like the country itself," she said. "Reality does not support existence of such a bushpig, and reality did not support the continued existence of the country." She turned the stamp around towards us. "In reality, a bushpig is anything but graceful. The jungles of South Africa have no place for such indulgences. The geopolitical climate of Africa also had no place for Bophuthatswana back then. It has an even lesser place for anything like it now."

"Go on," I said after she went quiet. "I don't know much about it and there is not much I could find."

"Have you seen the movie *Seven Samurai*? No? I have. And I love it. I know that doesn't fit the stereotypical definition of what you gentlemen feel a woman should like or not. I watched it a few years ago, and I continue to be impressed by how influential the movie has been. It affected popular culture, and it guided the conduct of a whole generation of managers in organizations. In the case of Bophuthatswana, I would like to think it was the case where a governing decision was inspired by the movie. The country was essentially a collection of seven regions."

"I am not in complete agreement with your interpretation," Mauna interjected. "Perhaps that had nothing to do with the movie. Perhaps it was just a coincidence, and maybe the movie and everything else you are impressed with has more to do with how the world has always been mesmerized with the number seven."

"Maybe. I like to believe my version is more interesting. It makes it so very non-trivial."

"It very much does," replied Mauna. "So many countries have appeared, and so many have disappeared in the last century or so alone, we need to proactively non-trivialize them all."

"Should we also non-trivialize each and every human who has ever lived within the last century alone?" Charesh jumped in. "But what I find most striking is that this process may not have ended. It may only have just started. I'll tell you what ... in our lifetime itself we'll enter the phase of consolidation of countries. You mark my words."

"You mean era?" I asked with a smile, half-jokingly trying

to enter the conversation. "Yes, yes, era," Charesh replied with a dismissive wave of his hand. "We are part of a massive unprecedented change in how human society is structured. This trajectory will not be reversed. It doesn't matter if many challenges pop up on more local time scales."

"Maybe," I said. "Time works on a scale we human beings cannot completely grasp. I find it very fascinating to imagine that a thousand years ago, in a similar setup, perhaps a group of people were engaged in a similar discussion. Or maybe a thousand years from now, who knows, a different version of us will be talking about the same things. Look at this stamp I have from Chad." I picked it up in its clear cover and passed it around. "I have not come across many triangle postage stamps, and this is the only one in my collection."

"I find them odd," Upalla replied. "In a world where stamps carry national pride and ego, I cannot quite understand the reasons why there would be so few of them. I have a stamp … here, let me pull it out," he proceeded to rummage through his collection. "Here. This is the smallest stamp in my collection. I think it's not any bigger than about 1.5 by 2.5 centimeters in size."

"Oh, a stamp from Southwest Africa!" Orphia exclaimed. "I love it! I've always been fascinated by that part of the world. I spent some of my childhood years there. If you don't know, it's now called Namibia. It was Southwest Africa when it was ruled by South Africa, which was not really much different than the relationship between South Africa and Bophuthatswana. Bophuthatswana was an attempt to legitimize apartheid."

"That's true," Upalla said. "The stamp is beautiful, indeed, but why so small? Or why would one have triangular stamps?"

"This is very interesting," Mauna jumped in. "I think it is trying to make a statement. I mean, Chad is as close to a failed state as can be. A triangular stamp may be its effort at a restart, perhaps to say to its citizens, and the world, that regular-shaped stamps represent a past we want to leave behind, and this triangular stamp proves it. Incidentally, I think Chad is surrounded by five or six countries, maybe the only country in the world to share the border with so many countries."

"No, I think Russia shares its borders with more countries," Orphia said.

"And I stand corrected," Mauna replied. "But speaking of everything being left to dust," he looked at me, "I think a few millennia ago, that place was all green and important. Now it's basically a desert."

"Wasn't it a French colony in the very recent past?" Charesh asked.

"I think it was," I replied.

"Yes, it was," Mauna responded.

"It's another one of those French problems," Mauna continued after a brief interlude when everyone was thinking of what to say. "I think the French were more problematic colonizers than the English."

"Were there any good ones? Any one you *miss* being ruled by?" Orphia asked with an exasperated look, as if ready to pounce with follow-up sarcasm to his response.

"No, there weren't, and it would be foolish of me to imply any support whatsoever for colonization. Brutality was at its heart and its ill-effects may take centuries more to completely play out. Hypothetically if, and only if—and don't misconstrue what I am trying to imply—even if imperfectly," he turned towards Orphia, "if freedom from colonization is not a choice, and the only given choice is to be colonized by the English or the French, I would choose the English. The French were slightly haughtier than the English. Not that the English weren't. It was just they were a bit more involved in and accommodating of the local cultures, while the French were willing to be a tiny bit more dismissive. This must have been the result of the lesson they learned from the American independence war, which is also perhaps why they ended up with the biggest empire in the world. You cannot run something on this scale by being aloof to local cultures. This difference has had some serious ramifications. But, I say, they were both better than Leopold for sure. He clearly played a big hand, with all seriousness and no pun here, in driving away humanity from the Congo. I can only hope it comes back and comes back soon."

"Hopefully," Orphia said with a drawn face, as she began flipping through her collection.

"But coming back," Upalla jumped in, "to odd-shaped stamps, there's definitely something odd about those stamps, or maybe their scarcity. I would say that countries would have let their imaginations run wild and shown off their creative impulses by coming up with different designs. You would have imagined an all-out stamp design war between the United States and the Soviet Union during the Cold War. But nothing like that happened. They were mostly regular shaped stamps, and mostly pretty dull."

"This is a very interesting observation indeed," Mauna replied.

"Very interesting," Charesh added. "I think it has perhaps something to do with the fact that postal work was always considered to be very serious and very dull work, with creativity playing only a limited role. Possibly, but just possibly, it may be a subconscious legacy of the mores of the era when the world revolved around writing, posting, and receiving letters, and a vocal public that preferred its stamps a certain way. Perhaps we all do mostly think alike and take comfort in some universally accepted order and have an aversion towards change. Maybe this is what humanity is, since Mauna mentioned it, but in a different context."

"Speak for yourself!" Orphia exclaimed with a smile. "This is all because it was a highly male-dominated work for so long. Women were not encouraged to be stamp collectors. I think if women had been more encouraged and involved there would have been a greater exploration of stamp designs."

"Perhaps. But not everything can be the fault of men, can it?" Upalla said with a slight raise of his eyebrows.

"No, but women have been particular targets of exclusion and discrimination by mere dint of being women," Orphia said with a lower and drier voice.

"And men have been particular targets of being expendable by dint of being men," Upalla smiled, as if sensing an opportunity to win an argument. "If young girls were snatched to keep soldiers in battles happy, young boys were snatched, too, from their mothers, forcefully conscripted, and sent to die in battles."

"There, there." Charesh waved both hands like a pugilism referee attempting to separate two boxers. "I said it before, society was structured a certain way, based on discrimination and exploitation taking on a certain form, where most people did not escape that paradigm. Most never escaped exploitation," he looked around at everyone, "some more so than others. We are undergoing a transformation, and we can see it all around us. Exploitation and discrimination will not go away, perhaps ever, but the paradigm defining them is changing. Awareness is increasing. Let's acknowledge and celebrate that truth. We're moving towards a different world."

"Hopefully!" Orphia replied grudgingly, while maintaining a cheerful tone. "I'll wait for that world. And," she turned towards Upalla, "we'll keep this topic for another day."

Mauna, perhaps sensing the sharpness in the atmosphere, eagerly jumped in and very conspicuously tried to steer the conversation away. "In all our discussions today, we, of all people, should not forget the role the lowly postal employee played in shaping the world. They connected the world, oftentimes on foot, one step at a time, sometimes on horse carts, sometimes on bicycles, braving rain, braving cold, or blazing heat, robbers, murderers, who knows what, and delivered. They were the emails and instant messengers of society. They brought us to this point."

"They, and the railway employees," Charesh said. "They built nations."

"They did, indeed," Upalla said. "Think of any country

tethering on collapse, and you can see a collapse of the postal system."

"Does anyone know what's going on in Afghanistan? Is there a reliable postal network covering the country right now?" I asked.

"I don't know. It's a good question. I still cannot get over the fact that those majestic Bamiyan statues were so wantonly destroyed," Mauna said. "The altar of religion demands stupidity and sprinkles tragedy. Interestingly, and since this talk about Afghanistan came up, I was reading about Ahmed Shah a couple of days ago, you know, the one who's considered to be the founding father of Afghanistan? He did a real number on India and Iran and other places. Just brutal. Many folks now consider his military campaigns as one guided by overwhelming religious fervor, but I don't think this is completely true. It's easy to mistake the present for the past, or even the future. Afghanistan is probably the one piece of cursed land in the world, and probably has been for thousands of years. The way it's sandwiched between different entities, it's always been the playground for powerful empires, and has also been very tribal in nature. I think Ahmed Shah did the only thing he could to assume control over the tribes, as barbaric and unforgivable as it was. And he wasn't the first one to try this approach. He gave the tribes the promise of huge spoils. But the weight of history is never inconsequential. His empire started collapsing even before his death, and quickly unraveled back into warring tribes. In spite of that, I think his role in shaping history on a global scale is much under-appreciated. How long ago was that? Only ten generations ago? We forget how recent so many important events of history took place across the vast expanse of time. And we ignore the heavy weight they bestow upon us. Anyway, I mentioned him because I thought you would find it interesting, and we were coincidently just talking about Afghanistan."

"Yes, it is interesting. I would like to know more when I can," Orphia said, and then turned towards Charesh. "You mentioned postal and railway employees and nation building. So, who are the nation builders now?" she asked.

"Yes, who do we call nation builders now?" I jumped in.

"They still are, I guess," Mauna said. "But now nation building does not entirely mean the same thing. What you were talking about was not really nation building as much as nation defining. Nations are built on the backs of very many, and destroyed at the hands of the very many, with many like us doing both, sometimes simultaneously."

Orphia lifted her arm slightly to look at the time on her wristwatch. She then very deliberately began gathering her collection.

"I think it's getting late. I should leave," she said.

Soon we all packed up and said our goodbyes. I passed by Orphia as I made my way towards my car outside the library.

"A great meeting today," she said.

"It certainly was!" I stopped and replied. "Are you going to be coming to the next one?"

"I am not sure. I'll have a better idea nearer the date. It's going to be a busy few weeks ahead for me. We are rolling out a new product, and I can already feel the stress and approaching misery." She smiled.

"How exciting!" I replied. "By the way, do you know of a Professor Bezbee? You might remember him from your college days, taking a course on artificial intelligence and using his book."

"Oh, those are not good memories!" She let out a small laugh. "But I vaguely remember something. Why?"

"Actually, he's visiting the university. He'll give a lecture open to the public this Thursday evening. I was wondering if you want to join me. I've heard he's a great speaker."

She thought about it for a moment, and replied, "Yes, why not? I think I would like it."

On Thursday, we met at the university parking lot. We had both arrived directly from work. Soon we were seated in a large auditorium, which quickly filled up.

Bezbee, on stage, from a distance, appeared to be of average height and modest demeanor. He became animated when he began talking, perhaps the result of having spent decades teaching something one is passionate about to captive classroom audiences.

The talk was initially a primer on his research accomplishments, with the opening humorous minutes spent recollecting his childhood fascination for robots and books by Asimov, which set him on his professional path. He talked at length on how the field of artificial intelligence has come a very long way. He then delved into the many possible futures for artificial intelligence.

"We have to understand, no matter what we say, and how we say it, that artificial intelligence is essentially playing with creating artificial life. Now whether that supplants us or supports us is a matter for debate, but its progress is not a matter of choice. Factory workers will be replaced. Desk jobs will be replaced. Soldiers will be replaced. Doctors will be replaced. Scientists will be replaced, even those working in this field. How many, and in what manner, we do not know. It all depends on how this field progresses. And it will also depend on what kind of a life we view artificial intelligence to be, and the language we use to describe it. Let me digress a bit and indulge in a bit of philosophical musing on the importance and evolution of contextualized language in rapidly shaping and reshaping the anthropomorphic, but culturally variant, value on life. We know that the last several decades, which is where I now focus, have seen an unprecedented destruction of the ecology and plunder of forest and ocean resources. Consider the conversion of meat into factory production. Or even consider the reliance of the global pharmaceutical and luxury industries on exploiting natural resources in one form or another. This has been possible because of technological advancements in fields as diverse as engineering and life-sciences. These advancements were in turn guided by an impetus, governmental or societal, and were exemplified in spoken and written languages. In China, it was the Great Leap Forward initiative. In India, it was the slogan to eradicate poverty and widespread food insecurity. In the West, it was personalization of the fear of a global population time bomb, for the need to win at all costs and on all fronts against a communist or capitalist competitor. This has changed significantly in just a few short decades. There is a greater understanding that all life is interdependent, even though we do not yet fully grasp this interdependency—one reason why all mosquitoes are simply not killed globally so as to prevent many terrible diseases. The earlier roots of this wider awareness again lay in the way language was used to qualify the many consequences of human developments. 'Loss of beauty,' 'the last untouched forest/space,' were some of the many expressions that made it into popular lingo in the West. In contrast, these have only recently started making their way into eastern societies on a wider scale. The juxtaposition of human experiences and lexicon on animal experiences has also been rapidly shaping this change. Koko the gorilla is the most extreme example you may know. That, along with a greater role that cats and dogs started playing inside individual homes, also helped cement an understanding that animals and, at least, big creatures of the sea such as whales and dolphins have complex emotions that can be described by simple words. Words such as 'sustainable' or 'organic farming' form an image of animals being treated with utmost care and love as would be understood by humans, able to enjoy freedom, right until the moment they are gently and painlessly harvested for food. This has in turn guided further developments in the fields of technology and biological sciences. Just as I grew up in an era where robots and artificial intelligence were the major innovations, we are now raising generations of scientists and engineers immersed in the zeitgeist of this era as defined by its language. We are, it appears, moving towards a gentler world with more, quote-unquote," and he did the irritating action with his fingers, which I too do, "intelligence. Now, I know, I know," he raised a hand towards the audience, "it does not look like it. It looks like a cruel world, where people are devalued, animals are devalued, plants are devalued, oceans are devalued, and the air is devalued. And most times it appears all our social and political leaders, and a vast majority of the masses, lack the intelligence or willingness, or both, to make things better. But I ask you, not as a counter-argument but as an exception, to not live in the moment. View the present only as a minuscule, infinitesimal slice of time, something that connects the past with all possible futures. You'll all get at least some sense of how the world has become less violent. One reason is perhaps we are very good at killing off amongst us those most prone to violence, and therefore, perhaps those who avoid violence among us are being genetically favored. Or we've made so much progress, and television has penetrated to the extent it has, that we find constructive outlets for our emotions, leaving less time for the pursuit of violence. Or perhaps, maybe, it's possible, that we are living in a time of unprecedented wealth, where many of our most basic needs are being met, at least for a sufficient number of us, so we collectively view large scale wars as a threat to that security. Possibly some future research may be able to shed light on this. And I have to end my talk on this positive sounding note, because there is no more appropriate way to end it. I have thoroughly enjoyed this, probably because I was the one doing all the talking!"

He died about a year later.

After the talk, Orphia and I went to a bar and restaurant near my home, a place I frequented. We had some deep-fried appetizers with our drinks. We talked about work and our lives, and before we said goodbye, decided on our next date.

Hans took me under his wings because once the laws of probability—his favorite phrase, not mine—had done their work, the outcome was certain. He was a successful man with a coterie of admirers always surrounding him. He was also handsome, which, if you ask me, supposing my opinion has any weight, which it does not at least to me, is always a strong indicator of a bright future. He certainly was bored with his present company and needed someone outside his normal circle to challenge him. When we met at the airport lounge, at the bar, waiting for our flights, I did not recognize him. I am not particularly given to being awed in the presence of position, fame, or success, and so I did not pay much attention to him or the people surrounding him in transparent obeisance. He seemed to have recognized me, though, and looked at me intently as he strode out of the lounge followed by the small troupe. A couple of minutes later, a man in crisp formal attire with shiny black leather shoes—the only real eye-catching feature about him—approached me. He introduced himself and mentioned that he worked for Mr. Ray. He then asked for my name. I hesitated for a moment and looked into his eyes, but without being able to discern his intentions. They looked uncertain, even judgmental. I gave him my name, and a respectful smile broke across his face, which was overshadowed by somewhat flailing hand gestures.

"Why do you ask?" I couldn't control my curiosity.

"Mr. Ray sent me to inquire. He said he was very certain, but wanted to confirm," he replied.

"And who is he?" I asked.

"Oh, you don't know Mr. Ray?" He seemed taken aback. In his world, it seemed, everyone knew Mr. Ray. "He was just here at this lounge. Did you not see him?"

I did not wish to make this conversation too long. "No, I did not. I wasn't paying attention."

"I understand. Unfortunately, he's had to rush to his flight. He just received permission for takeoff and it's a very small window. But he asked me to give you this," he pulled out a business card and gingerly handed it to me, "and requested that you give him your phone number, so he may reach out to you. If you'll be kind enough to give me your number, I can pass it to him."

I looked at the card very carefully. It had nothing but his name, Hans Ray, and his phone number on it. I had never seen a business card like this before. It was as if he expected you to know him, and if you didn't, then you didn't matter. I looked up at the man attempting to read his expression. I was met with the same dutiful smile, which had not changed, and must have been hurting him somewhat. I looked back at the card to try and make sense but couldn't. Fleetingly, I entertained the thought of this being an elaborate hoax or scam. I gave him my number with some hesitation because I did not want to be the one making the call. He noted my number carefully on a small notepad and repeated it twice to confirm. He then smiled broadly, from ear to ear, and proceeded to sprint out of the room with jubilation at a job well done.

I received a call from Hans Ray that very evening. He knew my name, he knew the village and the humble beginnings I came from. He knew my father, he knew my mother. He seemed to know everything. Finally, when I could no longer control my curiosity, I asked him who he was and what he wanted.

"Of course! How can I forget that you wouldn't remember!" He almost growled with excitement. "I am the *Swami* who lived in your village those many years ago. Do you remember now?"

I, of course, had not forgotten him. But him? Hans Ray? And who was Hans Ray?

"I am so very happy to see you all grown up," he said. "I thought I recognized you when I saw you at the airport. But so many years have passed. So many. How many? Twenty? I am now staring at old age, while you are still young. I have all the money and power one can imagine, but not the vigor. You, on the other hand, can drink to your heart's content, eat pizza as much as you like, and go out late into the nights."

"You have a misplaced idea of what it is to be my age." I smiled into the phone. "I have often wondered about you. You were a big influence in my life, maybe the only real one. You should not have left so abruptly. A goodbye was in order."

"Well, now it's time to say hello," he said. "Why don't you meet me? I will have my assistant call you to plan your trip. I'll try to keep a whole weekend open."

After the call ended, I did an internet search on Hans Ray. And I was dumbfounded. Hans Ray, the billionaire, the one who hobnobbed with leaders and rulers of countries, the one who was blamed for the collapse of the economies of a few countries, the one who was Chairman and CEO of a global investment company, an industry leader on the board of many companies, a well-known philanthropist. All this apparently within the last fifteen to twenty years.

"Do you believe in God?" he asked me. We were both seated in very comfortable chaise lounges on an elegant rooftop of a very impressive two-storied home, with a clear blue sky and gentle sun above us, idly staring at breaking waves just beyond the shoreline somewhere on the eastern part of the north island of New Zealand.

"I am not sure," I said, as I sipped a very fruity, orange, fine-tasting margarita. "I like to think I don't. I like to believe I am very rational, but I also like to think I am not completely and totally responsible for my life and its difficulties, that there's someone I can turn to, perhaps someone who makes sure that good deeds are appropriately noted and rewarded."

"I know what you mean." Hans turned towards me. "I know the feeling. I know. It's something to do with believing in the presence of an entity that gave us this life and gave us a purpose and perhaps even a destiny. That all our trials and hardships are for fulfilling that purpose and destiny … that it all has to matter."

"I suppose so." I took another sip, savoring the taste first between my lips, and then slowly swirling it around to all corners of my mouth.

"I am the one person who should believe in God," he said as he stared straight ahead. I eyed his untouched glass, wondering if he was going to drink his cocktail. I wasn't sure why he was denying himself the pleasure. But then, for someone of his stature, such pleasures were far too many and too easily available to hold any particular value.

"I should believe in the existence of God. I should believe that whatever has happened to me in my life so far has been the result of a benevolent yet stern God, someone who has silently guided me to where I am and will guide me to where I should be. And so, I should trust Him."

"I suppose so," I said again, and took another sip.

"But you know what," he turned towards me and looked at my now almost empty glass. "You are almost done! Did you like it? Want another one? Perhaps you should try the mojito this time. My bartender makes the best mojitos in the world." He pressed a small buzzer on the side of his chair. "She is a phenomenal bartender. I met her in Italy, I think. Yes, Italy. Danny, where did I pick you up from? Was it Italy or France?"

Danny was a tall, thin woman, probably in her late twenties, or at most, very early thirties. She exuded professionalism and maintained a facial demeanor that subtly prevented one's attention from moving away from her eyes, even when she was not looking at you.

"Or was it Spain?" she said, with a slight mischievous twitch of her lips as she looked at him.

"Oh yes!" Hans exclaimed. "I think it was Barcelona. It has been a long, long time. What year was it when you started working for me?"

"It has been a long eleven months, Sir," she replied, without changing her facial expressions.

"Alright, alright, no need for sarcasm. I told you I'll increase your salary when you make that perfect drink. Now be kind enough to make my friend here your famous mojito."

"Yes, Sir!" She turned towards me, smiled, and sauntered inside.

"Oh, don't worry about her." Hans looked at me with a broad smile. "We oftentimes banter. She is from Mexico City.

A very talented person who has learned a lot from her life struggles. I am paying for her part-time MBA at Harvard. I am also involving her in my business interests south of the United States. If she doesn't lose focus, she'll someday be a partner."

Danny brought me the mojito and went back inside. I took a small sip and found it hard to imagine any mojito better than this.

"I am a product of the laws of probability and statistics," Hans said after he watched me savor the drink. "So is Danny. And so are you. You may call those laws God, but I know what they are. Probability and Statistics are the true gods. They are the ones we have a personal relationship with. They work in mysterious ways, as much as your ignorance or limitations allow. Do you think she or I or you are particularly blessed to be leading the lives we are leading? Do you think I am more blessed than you, or that Danny is very blessed to have this Being lead me and my business associate to the hotel bar where she was working, and then make us both pay attention to her skills, which caused that associate to be in a better mood and more agreeable to my terms, eventually leading me to hire her?"

He glanced at me with a questioning look, which I took as him wanting me to play my role in carrying the conversation forward, because he was sure of the answer himself.

"A series of propitious events, I suppose," I said. "Maybe guided by God, maybe coincidences. Look, I am thankful to whatever has helped me, and I try to learn from whatever adversity I face. I don't think much about it."

"If she has been actively helped, then towards what end? I am sure she'll play her part in trying to make the world a better place, but I wouldn't count on it. I know enough. Wanting to make the world a better place is not a function of your station in life, but of the make up of your psyche," he said, apparently ignoring what I said. Perhaps it just came from his training in life, where he did not particularly have to respect the words of others. Most people he interacted with were already predisposed to choosing words to please him.

"I hobnob with enough people like me," he continued, "you know, billionaires and such, to get to know them personally beyond the public persona they project, especially their media personas. You know who all I am talking about." He smiled. I gave a slight nod of my head. I had no idea who he meant.

"I'll tell you what. People like me did not become people like me without being ruthless, and hardworking, selfish, and very, very lucky. Mostly very, very lucky. We, just like most people, try to help the world only as an afterthought, or not at all, just like so many others. We are no different. Just like Danny's life has been guided by probability and statistics, so will her desire to do something bigger."

"You almost seem to have a divine-like idea of probability. Maybe that's your God." I smiled.

"It is, oh, it indeed is." He smiled back. "Only this is not my personal God. This God is only guided by the rules of math. But I trust it more. I also fear it more. That's precisely why I am a successful investor."

Our view of the clear sky above was interrupted by a seagull, a hefty one, a mix of white, black, and yellow, as it passed us by. It spotted us and took a slight turn and gave a full-throated shrill caw. It came back, circling us again. After making a few rounds, the seagull hovered and then stared us down, most likely anticipating food. It gave another caw, and then another, as if provoking us to throw some food its way, a behavior it acquired from its many interactions with seaside visitors and tourists. A few moments later, alerted by this seagull, the view around was completely blocked by a horde of birds, mostly seagulls, but also a few ravens and what looked like sparrows.

"What do we do?" I asked Hans.

"Do? We enjoy the sight. But we don't feed them. The last thing I want is for my home to be a version of the Hitchcock movie *The Birds*. Have you watched it? One scary movie.

When these seagulls realize they'll not get anything from us, they'll go away."

He must have sensed I wasn't fully paying attention to his words.

"They're not too different from us, you know, these birds," he said. "We behave the same when we are hungry, or in want or need of something."

"I don't think this is correct," I interjected. "Maybe if you take the entirety of the behavior across all species of birds. I think we humans are something else. I think we carry the negativity and brutality of all the bird species combined."

"Wow, aren't you the cynical one." He smiled and turned towards me. I kept my eyes on the birds. I wasn't so much mesmerized by the sight, which I was to an extent, as I was concerned that one or some of them might decide out of desperation to swoop down and attack me and my drink. "You are right that I am guilty of treating non-human living entities as one big group. By the way, have you ever come across a kiwi? We should do a kiwi viewing tomorrow before you leave. One of the most territorial birds I know. They are so aggressive you'll be ensorcelled. I guarantee it."

The crowd of birds, meanwhile, began to thin out, undoubtedly realizing this was not their lucky place. Finally, one last remaining bird, (and it would have been a parodic touch if it was the same first bird), flew a complete circle above our heads, hovered briefly in front of us, and gave a shrill caw before taking off.

"That was something," Hans said. "An attitude! Now, where was I before we had these visitors?"

"Probability," I said, and took a long swig from my glass.

"Ah, yes, probability," Hans said. "These birds ruined the serious conversation we were having. Or perhaps not. Maybe it wasn't that serious. All I wanted to say was that what happens to us all is, to the largest extent, a set of lucky or unlucky happenstances, and our reactions to them. Our reactions are determined by our character, which is also shaped, maybe even determined, by the circumstances. Our very birth is shaped by chance, by the luck, good or bad, bestowed on a sperm cell and an egg. It could have very well been another sperm cell or another egg, and you and I would not be here. You can say that God wanted one particular sperm, out of tens of millions, to be the lucky one for that one egg, or you can say that one out of a few ten million sperms was lucky enough to overcome the odds. It's still the same, but with different emanations."

"And ramifications," I interjected. "Those two pictures are not the same. This reminds me somewhat of the weak anthropic principle."

"Yes, yes, I know what you mean. You have to allow for shortcomings in my speech because of the drinking. I am much older than you, and I have had nearly as much as you. What I meant was that the result is still a person who came to be because of one sperm cell out of tens of millions. Anyway, the gist of what I am trying to say is that my life has turned out the way it has, with an entitled upbringing, with an incorrect diagnosis of cancer, with the time spent in your childhood village, with the realization that one's life is too short and unworthy of taking seriously, plus the risks that I chose to take, they are all collectively responsible for me reaching here. I am where I am, because given all that has happened to me, it was not tremendously improbable that I became who I am. Now, let's head back inside and drink some more. Tonight, we will explore the night life here. I have wanted to do it for some time now. And with you here, I feel kind of young once more, at least for tonight. Come Monday, I have to get back to pretending to be sophisticated and powerful."

I never really fully understood why I ended up working for Hans. Perhaps he convinced me to join his firm. Perhaps he convinced me I would exceed expectations given the exorbitantly high salary he offered me. I was an engineer by training and felt I would be out of my comfort zone working for an investment firm, especially where my performance would be of interest to a multi-billionaire who also owned and personally ran the firm. But this was of not much concern to Hans. He promised me an extensive work-training period.

"You are an engineer," he said. "Most of these things will be easy for you, trust me. If you just apply yourself, and can handle cycles of protracted monotony and short bursts of overstimulation well, you'll excel. The world is scared of engineers. That's why they try to confine you to cubicles and put incompetent managers above you, or those who control the flow of money. We are scared because we know it's you who build this world, not us, and somehow if we do not confine you and reduce you to caricatures, we will become irrelevant."

"Someone like you? Scared?" I smiled. "And aren't you trying to do the same with me?"

"Of course, I am. Is it wrong?" he asked.

I couldn't answer that. I joined his company not only because of the money. I was also not like Danny to him, in the sense that she was a bartender before and continued to be a bartender after she joined him. He wanted me to leave something I loved, and work with him on something completely different, perhaps even tedious and uninteresting. I was like Danny to him in the sense that he wanted to surround himself with younger people and take them under his wings, a fate not uncommon among many successful older men. Perhaps I joined his firm not only because he convinced me, but also because of the flattery. He wore my defenses down over a couple of weeks through phone calls and emails. I think he wanted me to join him because I was the one link between his life before the village and his life after the village, and he could converse with me with a level of comfort that he could not with almost everyone around him. Despite our friendship, I did not forget my position and the respect owed to him, and I afforded him the liberty of being on call for him. Subtly, however, and on more than one occasion, I let him know that I did not belong to his coterie. I was simply there to help him connect with his past and make and save money for my future.

Hans married two years later. His wife liked me. I could not stand her. Her teenage son was a thoroughly self-obsessed brat, but a lovable one, one that you instinctively knew meant no harm to anyone. I could not stand him either. When I first met him, he had just turned vegan and was trying to habituate himself to sleep on a hard wood floor with only a sheet and a soft pillow, but no mattress or cushioning whatsoever. He claimed he had been inspired by the book *The Story of My Experiments with Truth* by Mahatma Gandhi. Thinking correctly that I was no longer as important for Hans as before, I left his company and was quickly picked up by a big bank. I could not stand that job either. At the bank, they sensed in me a talent I wasn't aware of, and I was pushed up the hierarchy to become a vice president of an important division. I think I was given the importance because I was unafraid of speaking up, particularly to authority, when others around me were much more reserved because of fear of retribution. This probably made me appear more authoritative, compassionate, and knowledgeable than I really was.

It was a late Friday morning when Hans called me and asked that we meet for lunch. Barring a very serious medical condition, or perhaps even then, one always showed up for meeting him at a place and time he decided.

"When you called me for lunch, I thought it was something serious." I remember trying to hide my boiling emotions.

"I am serious," he said.

"No, you're not. This is a joke."

"Yes, I am serious."

"Your family problems have got to you."

"I have no family problems."

"Then you must have fallen down and hurt your head."

"Come on. Listen to me."

"But I can hardly make sense of what you're saying."

"Let me explain again. And this time don't interrupt," he said. "Listen. I'll begin from the beginning, so you can understand the context. Until this morning, I was thoroughly, thoroughly bored in life, and of life. Sure, I know my wife's having an affair, perhaps multiple, and I don't mind talking to you about these things, you know that. Her son's okay, but he's also out of the home and doing who-knows-what at college. Forget all those things. Focus on the stock market. The stock market is my life, my reason for existence, my answer to the claim that life is meaningless. And for me, the past five months have been thoroughly miserable. Life no longer contains excitement or the feeling of adventure. And why is that? You know why! Do you not pay attention to the markets? You must know that the market index, after climbing up and falling down countless times, has now decided against doing anything at all. No doubt that prospect still holds roller coaster thrills for small traders, but for someone like me, there seems to be a void. Now it's true that the life of a stock trader does not necessarily need to be exciting beyond the stress of the market itself. And it isn't that I am not making money. For someone like me, the stock market is child's play. The point is, I am unable to make huge profits or take huge losses fast enough. Something that keeps the adrenaline flowing. That's what I am missing.

Now I want you to picture me from this morning. All depressed and haggard, forcing myself to get out of bed. I finally manage to reach my office and look at the market indices again and the prospectus and portfolios of a few companies, and I am ready to give up. I am ready to call it quits, bid farewell, and I am even considering going back to your village to spend the rest of my days. Really. I even contemplated simply walking out of my office, right then and there, and joining the hordes of people so many floors down on the streets. From my window they all looked happy, all moving around purposefully. That's when my administrative assistant, you know her, Nita, brings in a cup of hot green tea and a small chocolate muffin she baked the previous day for her family, and saved some for me. No, no, don't worry. I know what you are thinking. I am not calling it quits, and I am certainly not going back to your village. Listen, just listen. Let me complete my thoughts. Now, as Nita is leaving, she takes her cell phone and starts scrolling through it. That's when the idea came to my head. I asked her to get me the portfolio of a technology company I had come across a few days ago. I'd had her previously remove it from my desk because it had simply failed to catch my attention. But now I knew what I was looking for. This is a company, forget its name, it's not important, this is a company that is essentially a boutique app and services company, one that I would not bother with. What made me look at it again today was what gave me the idea I am here to discuss with you. First, going through the portfolio reconfirmed my original opinion. Here is a company trying to project, and project very forcefully and stylishly, that it's a big deal. But I know, I, with my experience, can see it very plainly, that it is doing nothing in particular. It's not that it doesn't have a core. It's that the core, and everything around it, is nothing, nothing in particular. What's more, regardless of my opinion, this company will still raise a lot of money in the market. That's when I knew what I wanted to do, wanted to try, before I take a complete retirement. I want to open a company, a huge company. A huge company with millions in assets. But a company with only four or five employees. The only focus of this company is to sell its stocks."

"You mean, the company focuses on stock trading, right? Which is partially what you do. That clears up everything. You need a loan for that? No problem. I am sure I can convince my people to give you a loan at a great rate. I wonder, though, why you'd open up another company to do what you're already doing," I interjected after trying a few times to get my voice through.

"Oh, how in this world did you become a big guy in such a big bank? Hear me out. What I mean is that the company's product is its own stocks. Get it? The purpose of its employees is to focus the market's attention on its stock, and take care of necessary paperwork and advertisements. Then the market takes care of everything. Listen, we have enough to gamble big and not worry about any losses. And life has been getting a little dull lately, anyway. Why not try something interesting?"

"But—"

"There's nothing illegal about it. It'll be a perfectly legitimate company. It has a product—its stocks. And it's not going to conduct itself illegally. I'll be its principal stockbroker, and you'll be its principal bank."

I sighed. I had to sigh.

Hans shot me a condescending look and replied calmly, "There's nothing wrong with the idea. Ask me any questions and I'll answer them. I've worked out some of the details, the rest we can address together. Now, wipe your face first. Your lunch has missed its mark by a good distance. Call your office and tell them you'll be late. Go to the restroom if you want while I order some coffee. I don't want any interruptions once we start."

Several weeks later a one-page advertisement in a leading business daily read:

Attention all Honest and Hardworking
Workers of the World

For hundreds of years, people like you have been exploited while people at the top have had a far too comfortable life for far too long at your expense.

Do you feel you're at the bottom rung at work? Do you feel you're struggling too much to make decent living? Do you wish you could have some say in the way things are, to even have some authority over the people who have controlled you for so long?

Last but not least, do you want to make money?

If you answered yes to these questions, then RE, Inc. is the answer. This is the first and only company in the world dealing in its own stocks. Employees of this company have only one duty: to make sure its stock has the highest value. The company has no other product except its own stocks. This means you get all the benefits of being a customer of a world-class company, while at the same time you have the power as a stockholder to influence and control the management.

Yes! By buying RE, Inc. stocks you immediately get three important benefits: You are treated as an important customer. You are treated as an important stockholder. And you get to exercise power that is rightfully yours.

So, what's stopping you? Don't wait—buy our stocks! Let the world know you matter! The employees of RE, Inc. are waiting to serve you now!

I was not a happy man. The reason was the stock market. I couldn't understand how I'd let Hans talk me into this crazy scheme. A month had gone by since the stock first entered the market, and now the shares weren't even worth the paper they were printed on. To top it all off, Hans was projecting the impression that he was quite happy with the way things were.

Losing a few million wasn't the problem. The problem was that I had become a laughingstock to those around me. None of my peers could believe that someone with any acumen could enter into so stupid an enterprise. The only reason I still had the job was because Hans was involved too. It wasn't easy to overlook this when thinking of firing me. But I was under no illusion. I would lose my job soon. There must always be a fall guy. I was the most obvious and convenient one.

One day, as I stared out my office window, feeling forlorn, contemplating leaving everything behind and spending the rest of my life in my village, my cell phone rang with a restricted number. I picked it up.

"Yes?"

"How are things today?" Hans's voice came from the other end.

"How are things with you?" I asked.

"You don't sound happy. Well, we'll talk about what ails you later. I just called to let you know that the second phase of our plan is coming into play shortly. Keep track of the stock market starting tomorrow morning."

"What is this second phase? You never told me anything about any second phase," I said, confused and concerned.

"Oh, really? Well, I must have forgotten," he answered blithely. "But don't worry. Look, I need to get off the phone now. I'll get in touch with you soon. Meanwhile, don't forget. Tomorrow morning."

The regulatory body came down, and came down hard, on us. I and a few others were arrested. We could not have been accused of a Ponzi scheme because it wasn't, though the prosecutors worked with the media to project just that to the public. We almost went to prison for insider trading, because a member of a royal family in a country, who had invested quite a bit, first tried to take over the company, and when that failed, took on a mission to destroy the company using whatever means, including physical threats to Hans's friends and their families.

It so transpired, which I only became fully privy to while trying to defend myself in court, that after his call to me on that fateful day, Hans made another call to another friend. Their conversation didn't last more than a couple of minutes. That friend then made calls to multiple people in quick succession, and those people made more calls. All these chains of calls terminated at brokerages, who immediately placed orders for stocks for RE, Inc. Consequently, by the end of the day people started to pay more than just a passing interest in the new company. By the end of the next day, the stock price had risen exceptionally high and continued to rise the day after that. Two weeks later, all the leading business dailies and magazines were talking about RE, Inc. and its single revolutionary idea. Not just people in the upper echelons of business, but ordinary working people were now taking a huge interest. And ordinary working people were now scrambling to buy the stock that would finally give them the power they felt they deserved.

In the end, so much noise had been created, so much negative publicity had been generated, that the inevitable happened. I lost my job and I also spent a year in prison on minor charges. I came out rejuvenated and determined to leave that life and the associated affluent lifestyle behind. I disposed of my expensive properties, consolidated all my money in long-term deposit accounts, moved to another city, and joined a company there as an engineer. I found that job through an old friend. Given the number of years I had been away from mind-paralyzing, but very satisfying real technical work, I had to start from nearly the bottom of the ladder. My friend had felt embarrassed in suggesting this position because at one point I was, according to him, someone he looked up to as a role model and inspiration. But this was just fine with me. I was not in any financial difficulty, and I was back to doing something I loved, or perhaps was more comfortable doing. My new position also involved less interaction with people, and less pretense. I am certain he must have secretly, or not very secretly, snickered at my fall. Everyone has a right to indulge in schadenfreude, and I am not one to deny anyone that pleasure, even myself, when the opportunity presents itself. I started my work enthusiastically, and less than a year later also took up a more-or-less semi-permanent residence in an apartment complex, with an apartment on a far corner of the property. All-in-all, it was a life of voluntary quietude. That is, until Anita showed up.

The only thing I heard about Hans at that time was that he left the city, with no further information concerning his whereabouts. About a year or so later, a childhood friend, one who kept in close touch with our familial village, told me about the village temple receiving a substantial donation and renovation from an old man who claimed to have known me. The man would spend all his days, and many a night, sitting quietly and often praying. One evening, he asked to be allowed to spend the whole night at the inner sanctum. They let him in and locked the main doors. In the morning, when the doors were opened, he was nowhere to be seen. He had, they said, disappeared into thin air, leaving no trace behind.

Chapter Four

the universe expands to connect with other universes

In my mind, they were always two different women—Orphia and Anita. They were one, but they were two. Or more. Perhaps more. I think they were more. I am sure they were more. I remember her always closing all the curtains at nine at night, every night, taking off all her clothes, and walking around the apartment completely naked. Yes, that's what she did. The sex, whenever it happened, was almost always never as exciting as I now think it should have been. Was it because she had never had an orgasm? She was probably incapable of having one. She told me and assured me it wasn't because of me. I remember her, the first time we almost had sex, she had knocked on my door, very late and very drunk, and said she wanted it wild. And then she proceeded to define what her definition of wild was. We did not do it. I took her to my balcony, gave her a glass of water, and then took her for a short walk before dropping her back to her home. I remember the conversation we had when she had broken up with her fiancé. It was a mild winter evening, and dark, when she pointed to her apartment and said, as a matter of dull fact, that she was going to have a lot of sex there. And she proceeded to do just that. I wasn't part of those acts. A couple of months later when we met, she, again as a matter of fact, told me she had had so many men that she was bored with them. Very briefly, during our conversation, she considered experimenting with women, just for a change, but decided against it because she found the idea of sleeping with women yucky.

In the end, whether she was Orphia or Anita, or someone else, or many different women, this is how I want to remember her. A new relationship, one that is not burdened with time, is one where all facets are exciting, worthy of exploration.

My work schedule was very comfortable. It allowed me to organize myself in a way that made my life as stress-free as it could have become. I could have had an even more stress-free life if I had simply decided to not work but just live off my savings and investments. But I needed to work. I think most people want to work, and most people want to complain about work, or anything that pays their bills. The idea that giving poor people money or assistance to help them through tough times, the belief that these handouts will make them lazy, is very misleading and cruel. Some of the laziest people I've ever come across have been the very rich. Some of the most crassly, dismissively cruel people I've known have been the very rich.

As I said, my life took on a different type of comfort, one that was deeply satisfying and fulfilling. I would wake up around nine-thirty in the morning, reach my office around eleven, work for about three hours without a break, head back home for lunch and a nap, hit the gym for an intense workout, or instead take a stroll if my body was aching from the previous day's workout, have a good dinner, head back to my office for a few more hours of work, and then go to my neighborhood bar for exactly three beers, before returning home and going to bed around two-thirty at night. This almost never changed, even over the weekends or holidays.

Soon, the bar became the focal point of my life. This became the place where, over a duration of ninety or so minutes, I could unwind, talk to random people and listen to their life stories, or just watch them get drunk and have a good time. I would return from there rejuvenated every night. I would wake up in the mornings with the knowledge that no matter what the day would throw at me, I would have a good ninety minutes at the end. Looking back, I think there was also an element of conceit and smugness to this, though I am very certain I did not outwardly demonstrate it, and even consciously realize it enough to acknowledge it. This was no upscale bar, with most of the customers coming from the lower to lower-middle strata of society. Some of them were certainly just a minor accident or mishap away from an unforgiving spiral into misery. These were the people I talked to, and talked with, and laughed with every day. Mostly I listened to them, and sometimes tried to lead their lives vicariously. Their troubles and tribulations were always a reminder to me on how we all lead similar lives when it comes to our joys and our sorrows. But more important, I could always take solace in how small my life-issues were compared to theirs. I always made it a point to not talk about my troubles and issues with others in the bar. My life did not matter. Theirs did. They were already providing me company. People there knew I was well-off, and knew I was a friend of Ron, the bar owner—someone who was known for being friends with people who had money. He was a slightly overweight older man, in his mid-to-late-sixties at that time. Sometimes he looked older and sometimes he seemed younger, depending on his disposition on any given day. Years of heavy drinking, smoking, and eating, with no physical exercise, had taken their toll. Two bitter divorces did not help either. But he was a man of some honor. From what I knew, he had in all these years, never hit on any of his female employees, no matter how drunk he or they might be. He respected everyone who worked for him and paid them well, earning their respect and admiration, and even affection from some of them. He was now lonely and rich, with mostly the people at the bar—the customers, the bartenders, waiters and waitresses, and bouncers—his real company. This was not much different than my life, I suppose. The one difference was that, while for him the bar was his life, for me, it was only a part of it. I was mildly addicted to the place, no doubt. But I could just as easily walk away from it, and he could not. My addiction to the bar, so to speak, did not stem from my liking the drinks. Drinking was never central to my life and I never craved alcohol. The bar provided me a comfort zone, which made me come night after night.

It was what is called a speed bar, geared to serving large crowds with beer and easy-to-mix drinks. It was a friendly bar with a welcoming environment where the drinks were cheap and therefore affordable to the customers it served. This also attracted a sizable number of students from the near-by university, which in turn would make the place crowded and boisterous at times. The bar was fairly spacious, and had undergone many changes on the inside, many of them done by Ron himself with his own hands. The building was not a marvel of architecture by any measure and had a rundown exterior and several dilapidated areas inside. Ron knew the type of crowd this place catered to very well and avoided any ostentatious fixes and upgrades, because they would almost always be damaged in a short time. He went to the extent of affixing a large, thick, white piece of wood, covering almost the entire wall, over the urinals in the men's room. This was done to let drunk men satisfy their craving of carving things on walls, without damaging the wall itself.

Inside, the bar had two separate sections. One was the pub part, the part with wide-screen televisions almost always tuned to different sports channels, and there were also pool tables, a jukebox, and other games. The other part had the dance floor with its own separate bar, where an eclectic mix of music would play. Some nights would be karaoke nights. There was also the outdoor patio for those days when the weather was good or the karaoke was bad. I always confined myself to the former space. I would enter and seat myself on a high stool by the bar, facing the two television sets. The bar extended from a small refrigeration room at its back and faced a fairly open area with the pool tables and other games on one side, and dart boards on the other, and the jukebox on the far wall.

In just a few short weeks of going there regularly, I reached a level of familiarity with the bartenders such that I did not even need to order my first beer. My beer would be brought and placed on the tabletop in front of an empty high stool as soon as I was seen entering the premise. Eventually, I did not even need to give my credit card upfront to open a tab.

The first person I got to know there was a young bartender by the name of Chelsea. She was twenty-five when I first walked into the place. Self-proclaimed overweight, the result of a few years of a good amount of drinking and eating a fat-rich diet as she claimed, she was off the mark concerning her opinion of her weight. She was also very quick, efficient, and meticulously clean. She introduced me to others at the bar, including Ron, the owner, and at times took upon herself the responsibility of keeping me comfortable, saving me from interacting with questionable characters, and sometimes saving some food and cheese for me. Ron would occasionally, sometimes even a couple of days a week, cook easy to grab and eat things for customers to dive into. This would usually be some meat or chili, taco rolls, and shredded cheese. If you were there early enough you could make yourself a taco or two, or more, and have them with your drinks. For me the biggest draw was the cheese: specifically, shredded cheese sprinkled on popcorn. The popcorn was always cooking, every day, in the popcorn machine. Since I used to arrive late, Chelsea would keep some of the cheese on the side for me. She was living with her boyfriend Daniel, a short, stocky and slightly rough, balding man, about ten years older than her. We got along well whenever he dropped by at the bar, which in the beginning, was very often. He was working as a cook at a nearby restaurant with late hours and would be there to pick her up at closing time, which was two in the morning. When the restaurant closed permanently, he found work with a construction company. This came with a grueling work schedule, requiring heavy physical labor and a need to be on site early mornings, irrespective of what the weather planned.

But it paid well and kept him happy. It also meant that he stopped coming to the pub, except on weekends. And on the weekends he would help out behind the counter when things became busy. I never found out how good and quick he was at mixing drinks, but he could certainly open very many beer bottles in just a few short seconds.

Chelsea, like so many there, workers and customers alike, had a good bit of mixed up family, the result of a couple of generations of societal changes where physical mobility and relationship fluidity became part and parcel of life. Her grandmother from her father's side had moved here from Denmark and lived nearby. The grandmother never got along with her or her siblings and mother's side of the family, and was largely ignored. Chelsea's father had married her mother at a young age, when he was still a college student and she was unsure of what she wanted to do in life. Later, when he became a doctor, he left his wife and children to move in with a younger, ambitious woman with career potential. They didn't stay together for long, and he never had a serious relationship after that.

It was not just Chelsea's father and grandmother who were lonely. The world has many older people who are lonely and oftentimes bitter. Part of the reason is an inability of society to determine what to do with old age. Society is very clear on how childhood and youth should be handled, and a great bit of resources are directed there. Adulthood is where one is defined by one's work and valued for an ability to generate resources and wealth, a return on investment made on the childhood form. But after this, after a certain age, and sometimes after society has determined it has extracted from one all the value it can, what next? Medical science is working diligently to prolong life, with great success. Human society has unfortunately not evolved quickly enough to find meaning in those many, many extra added years. Another reason was a mutinous bugle call by society to break the powerful and suffocating grip of patriarchy in its myriad forms. In many cases, this resulted in a shift in focus of responsibility from the collective to the individual and a concomitant drift towards an extreme form of individuality. In its wake has been left a sizable number of people who grow up emotionally stunted, unable to make any real connections with others, but always, always, struggling in their own ways to try. Unfortunately, they grow old before they succeed. I felt that Mike, a regular bar customer in his late twenties, well-built and always ready to break into a smile, was heading towards that future.

Chelsea's mother ended up becoming a hairstylist and, with family support, led a relatively comfortable and easy life. It is likely that Chelsea was inspired by her. She became a bartender and, at some point, decided that being a bartender here was the life she was going to lead and nothing more, the potential that her intelligence and work ethics had placed on her be damned. She also, as she once mentioned, hated reading, and did not read any books. There are many people who have an almost pathological fear of reading, a bibliophobia. She was not the first intelligent person I have come across to dislike reading. She was afraid to be exposed to thoughts and ideas that might challenge her notions about life. Her brother, though, perhaps had something to prove to his father. He got a medical degree from a prestigious medical school and joined a big hospital.

However, another bartender, Paloma, did not have the acumen for higher education. But she was astute, and no less perceptive than anyone else. She was a bartender because Ron paid her well and she instinctively knew, which she never failed to mention, that she would never get anything approaching this no matter where else and how hard she worked. She was in her mid-twenties, short, and, like Chelsea, quick on her feet and efficient. She assumed a commanding stature much taller than her physical self and did not mind berating an inebriated, demanding customer from time to time, or rolling her eyes to show her displeasure. Women working at the bar were never the overtly stunning fashion-ramp model-types, as one might find in many impersonal bars and pubs. They were never even required to dress in ways that objectified them. But they all had distinct, striking demeanors and personalities and attractive smiles, which exuded warmth, and which added to the welcoming charm of the place. Paloma was no exception. The early days of our meetings were ones of reservation from her side. For Paloma, I was a paying customer, albeit a regular one, but still just a paying customer. Those were also the days when she was looking for a boyfriend and would unabashedly declare to those she knew, whenever she could, loudly enough, how she hated her single status. At some point, over the course of a year or so, she found a boyfriend, a man about fifteen years older than her who was divorced. He had a two-year-old daughter and shared joint-custody with his former wife. Both mother and daughter lived in a nearby city. He was a decent man, tall, balding, a survivor of a life-threatening illness, and a dedicated medic. His shifts were almost always afternoon-to-night, so every night that Paloma would work, he would show up. He usually sat in a corner, drinking beer and reading novels on his smartphone or playing darts with others. Occasionally he would be joined by a friend and colleague: younger, muscular, broad-chested, and good looking. He once had a very attractive girlfriend who had followed him from another state. I had met her on a couple of occasions when they both sought my advice on a career decision she needed to make. But they broke up when she discovered he was cheating on her. This was not a surprise because he was never bereft of female attention. There aren't as many good-looking men in this world as there are women, especially good-looking men with a steady job and potential.

The transition from just another paying customer to someone Paloma could confide in as a friend happened for reasons I don't fully understand. Perhaps she became more agreeable after she found a boyfriend, thereby feeling secure. Perhaps she also realized that I was not going anywhere else, that I maintained a sense of dignity and distance, and perhaps she saw that I became friends with Ron and many others. I had no hesitation in leaving large tips on occasions or buying drinks for those who worked there regularly as a genuinely felt sign of appreciation, and I always acted friendly. Paloma's family story was somewhat similar to Chelsea's. Both had well-to-do and professionally accomplished fathers who had left their wives, who were not nearly as educated, for younger women. In her case, though, Paloma's father did end up marrying his younger muse. This created more drama in her now extended family, with lots of acrimony and caustic comments. Oftentimes, when she was a customer at her own bar, seated on the other side of the counter and drunk, she would describe in varied details the latest happenings in that soap opera. Many times, she just descended into an endless loop of jumbled talk, which was, nonetheless, fun to listen to.

Jack was the other main bartender and also the manager of the establishment. This was his second job. He also had a daytime job running a shop or some such thing. Between the two jobs, he made a very comfortable living. He was also gay. He had a mother who worked part-time in another city and stayed with his two siblings. His younger brother was in college. His other sibling was a stay-at-home mother. Beyond this, I never learned much about his personal life. He was not one to open up easily. Or perhaps he was. I never found out.

There were others, too, but never anyone who stayed very long. Madison was a bartender and a student at the university. She became pregnant before she could obtain her degree and left work. I do not believe she had the means and support to complete her education and I did not hear about her again. Ed was another bartender I got to know briefly. He moved back to his hometown with his girlfriend, who had a degree in biology but worked a menial job at a local store. Ed, too, had a college degree. Born in another family with means and in surroundings different than what they both had known, I am certain they would have done very well, simply from exposure to different ideas and opportunities. Perhaps they have by now. But at that point in time, I found them both lost and trying to make sense of their worlds, afraid to take big leaps, both in physical space lest they lose their family support, and in career because of a lack of confidence emanating from the feeling that success is reserved for others, others already more successful, richer, happier.

One of the most interesting people to work there was a bouncer and doorman by the name of C. Over the three or so years I visited the bar, I had met three bouncers. All three were big, burly men, capable of lifting an average human over their shoulders without any effort. The first one, whose name I do not remember, had a long, thick beard, which he was very passionate about. He had a child from a previous marriage. When we first met, he had a girlfriend who was there with him regularly during evenings. At some point they broke up and his life spiraled downwards. Or perhaps she left him because he couldn't handle his life. In any case, after she left him, he started working somewhere else, and soon took to a life of petty crimes and drugs. He came in once as a customer, clean shaven, perhaps as a sign he was trying to put his life back on track. But this was short-lived.

Ethan was the other bouncer, a student at the university, a well-proportioned tall man with a charming, outgoing personality. He had poor control over his urge to flirt with any and all women, which clearly did not go down well with his girlfriend at the time, a quiet studious young woman who worked as a waitress at the bar as she paid for her education. Ethan came from a place that was once a hotbed of overt racism and was now a hotbed of covert racism. But Ethan, being Black, never showed, even when very drunk, that he was affected by racism. In that sense, he was somewhat like me, and we got along well together. If there was anything he could get out of you—knowledge, wisdom, information, or a drink, anything—he would talk to you, no matter who you were. He was very clear about what he wanted out of life, which was to get into a respectable profession and make a lot of money. He wanted to get an advanced degree in psychology and become a psychiatrist. I don't know if he ever became one. After he graduated, he worked as a salesperson in a chain jewelry store. For a while he was very happy with the salary he was earning. Last time I talked to him, he was still burning with ambition, and while happy with the job, had decided to leave it and move back to his hometown to pursue something different.

C wasn't exactly muscular. He was certainly very over-weight, and took his time carrying his weight around when he walked. But he was tough, very tough. You would not mess with him. If Hitler showed up at the bar, and you had this one chance to suckerpunch him and kick him hard when he went down on the floor, you would not do it with C around. No one wanted to create any trouble, no matter how justified or righteous, around C. If he asked you to put your unfinished drink down and walk out of the building at the close of the bar, you did just that, with a smile, after thanking him pro-fusely. But he was mostly very quiet and was rarely, if ever, loud, even when happy or excited. When he first joined, he was indubitably the worst pool and dart player that perhaps ever existed. But he played, nonetheless. Sometimes he played because he was invited to join by customers, and sometimes he played because there weren't any customers, except for me. There were times when, during weekdays when it rained hard or was cold, I would be the only paying customer in the bar. I would sit there, talk to anyone who was working, waiting for Ron to show up to close up. Ron usually arrived between one and one-thirty. As soon as he would arrive, he would be served what was called Ron-water, which was vodka with sweetened lime juice and lots of ice. He would then proceed to walk around talking to people, and more often than not, slowly make his way to sit down beside me. His daily routine was one reason why the bar was so successful. He gave it a more personal touch. You were not there just to drink, but to be part of a circle of companions.

C eventually became a good pool and dart player, and soon became a nightly fixture among the regulars. During days, he worked at a fast-food restaurant. Both jobs kept him busy. He needed two jobs because he was saving up to go to university to get a degree in English. C was, on the inside, completely opposite to his external persona. He was a very sensitive man, and one who was at peace with his turbulent emotions. He had a love for verse. He loved to read poetry, and he loved to compose poems. He wanted to attend university so he could immerse himself even further. When I first found out about this passion of his, I asked him to show me some of his works. I do not have a knack for poetry appreciation, but I was interested to see his work. The next night he brought two of his compositions. They were good, at least from the perspective of a layman like me. The next night, he brought a couple more. I read those, and we talked about them. I gave him some advice, with the caveat that I was not well-versed in the art. He did not seem to mind, and joyfully took my suggestions. I think I was the first person who had willingly, out of my own volition, shown interest in his work. I later learned that he had a collection approaching nearly a hundred poems. His oeuvre, so to speak, while vast and impressive, had one common theme: death. They weren't elegies, though, or eulogies for that matter. He covered death in its myriad forms, whether physical death, death of a relationship, death of innocence, death of pop culture icons. I am not sure why he was so dark. Maybe it had to do with being the oldest sibling in a broken family. His father was missing, and he never talked about him. His mother, according to him, was one who could not stand being alone and always needed a man in her life. This did not particularly surprise me. Going to the bar every night brought me in proximity of men and women who could not stand being alone. In many cases this was a manifestation of a desire for finding someone who could take control. In his mother's case, she found someone who took complete charge, and then some. He was an abusive man and she was a willing participant, one who was quick to make excuses for him, and unwilling to step up for her children. C left home and moved a thousand miles away, as far as he could, and brought along with him a deep regret of not being able to protect his family from the abuse. For a while, he stopped talking to her, too. It was death at many levels for him and it poured out on paper. But I think, or perhaps I like to believe, that his poetry reflected an underlying hope. His poems were the funeral pyre and he was the phoenix.

Shelby was the other interesting person, sometimes bartender, sometimes waitress. As unpretentious as she was serious, she was the mother to a toddler. She had a talent for being able to easily change her persona between the blithesome to the slightly astringent matron, maybe even without her knowing. I am not certain what her husband did, or how she could maintain such odd, late hours, working and occasionally drinking. She was a good, caring mother who doted on her child. I could never quite figure out why I found her interesting.

Grant and Jack, regular customers, or the in-house comic book heroes as I liked to call them, were co-owners of a four-year-old comic bookstore. They had moved the location of the bookstore to one near the bar about two years into their ownership. That's the time they started dropping in regularly. Perhaps the comic book heroes were the ones who created Anita, a comic book princess, and released her for me. Or Anita was a natural or preordained outcome of our meetings. It has to be the latter. I also don't believe she could have desired and committed her own creation. It doesn't work this way. There was the in-house lesbian group too, at least for about a couple of years before they were carried away by their individual lives. There was no in-house gay men group. Women, gay or straight, are now much more comfortable and vocal about their sexuality. Men are still struggling. The in-house genius was TP who, I am sure, knew more about electronics and computer systems than many professors at the university. He certainly knew more about so many things in the field than I did, even though my work was in the broad area, and at the cutting-edge. He was crazy I think, medically speaking, if that's the way to put it. But we've been told that there's only a thin line separating genius and crazy. I never knew what he did exactly, and how he earned his living. He wasn't someone of great means, but in that bar, one could never be sure. What I could gather was that he was most likely a freelance technical consultant or expert. He did a lot of work with people in Korea and Japan, and never failed to mention that they loved him there. We enjoyed each other's company whenever he would show up, which was not too often, and would work diligently towards getting very drunk. We had never actually met when he wasn't inebriated, which I think was my loss. Very drunk, he would be loud, though a happy loud, but would be loud enough in saying things that are best kept low key, if said at all. And like many who get very drunk, he would go into a conversational loop, repeating over and over again any topic he started. He would call me his brown terrorist friend and I would have to return the favor by calling him my KKK Neo-Nazi friend. It's not difficult to see why people around us would be offended by this kind of conversation. Walid certainly was. He was from the extended royal family of a Middle Eastern country. I wasn't offended, but I would tell him to temper it down whenever he became too loud, reminding him that he was making the bartenders and customers uncomfortable. I am not easily offended by prejudiced behavior at the personal level. I think that part of me, the part that should be offended, is damaged. I simply do not see the point in trying to interact with anyone who would not interact with me because of how they superficially perceive me. This is also why I was able to enjoy the company of a widely eclectic mix of people, politically correct or not, in both my professional and personal circle, people who would seek out my company and look up to me. Grant once called me an alpha male, and I retorted that I cannot be one because I don't have women around me. I am neither a leader nor an alpha male nor any such thing. People around me know very well that I address them as human beings, and human beings only. What I cannot stand is snobbishness. That to me is a greater fault than racism. A snobbish person carries nearly all varieties of prejudices known, and then some, and is unafraid of some part of his façade showing it. TP, though, was not prejudiced in his daily actions, but was certainly poor at telling race-based jokes when drunk. However, he felt compelled to make them anyway as a way of endearing himself to me. He talked to me as an equal, enjoyed my company, and debated and conversed with me on topics ranging from politics to religion. I did not mind telling him when he went too far or became too loud with his puns and jokes. I do not have a way to read someone's mind. Even mine. For all I know, I could be highly prejudiced myself. Actions and words are what count. And perceptions too. It's only a slippery slope if one perceives it to be. His friend Jason was open to entertaining prejudiced ideas. He was willing to be led down those paths if a leader provided the excuse and cover. TP would need to be forced to. TP was particularly interested in taking a long road trip with me to introduce me to Americana, stopping or boarding at villages and very small towns on the way. I wasn't particularly interested. I've lived in them enough.

Walid, a very thin man in his late twenties, was my first customer friend. We met when the bar was at a low point in daily customers, and there were enough opportunities to be introduced to different people. He had an outgoing and unpretentious personality that made him popular. He was also close to Ron, and that's how Ron and I became close. Walid had no hesitation in approaching and talking to people. At one point, he also had no hesitation in sending pictures of his private parts to women, dick pics as they are known in popular lingo. Not to all of them, of course. He had some very close women friends whom he treated with great love and respect. But when he sent a picture to a woman who was with Grant, while he was driving her back home from the bar, Grant decided to have a heated public discussion about it the next day. We all had a good laugh, and I think Walid never repeated it.

Many people did not like Walid, and many could not stand him. Paloma hated him. It wasn't simply a supercilious attitude. Perhaps because of his weight, Walid would get inebriated very quickly. But quite miraculously thereafter he would reach a sort of plateau in how much more drunk he could get. In that state he would go into a conversational loop and would refuse to come out of it. Many times, he would not make sense, and sometimes he would say and do borderline inappropriate things. Alfredo once told him that he, Walid, could be a robot programmed to believe he was human, and maybe we all could be, and Walid spent nearly an hour explaining loudly in my ears how he wasn't a robot. He also tried to describe how his religion viewed humans and went on to explain how he loved his religion. He once absentmindedly played with the bra straps of a woman while talking to her, with her boyfriend angrily watching, and one time he howled "nice ones" across the bar to a woman wearing a scandalously low-cut dress. But he was Ron's friend, the first friend-in-need whenever he needed one. He would spend hours with him, at his home. Ron let him keep a tab at the bar. In two short years, Walid's tab went to nearly fifteen thousand dollars. That's also when his parents in his home country stopped sending him more than the bare minimum amount of money, to force him to complete his studies and come back with his degree. But Ron didn't show any overt concern. He placed a limit on how much Walid could spend at the bar on any given day. He would sometimes cross the limit by getting drinks from others. Walid was somewhat of an incongruity or paradox in that place, a product of the dichotomy of the religious mind created by the tensions between demands of tradition and demands of the desire to fit in, in the present situation in life. He knew he had a few short years before he was expected to lead a very conservative life, and he was going to live it to the hilt. He would indulge in whatever was not allowed back home. Yet, at the same time, he held deeply traditional views, patriarchal views even, and accepted without question the prevailing political opinions emanating from his country. He was very happy living the somewhat wild life here, in fact was thoroughly enjoying it. I am more than fully sure that he would also be very happy, with no regrets whatsoever, living back home and leading the traditional life expected of him. The transition would be instantaneous, and the past life quickly forgotten. Maybe that's why he would come to this bar. It provided him the opportunity to be personal and familial, without worrying about the burdens and consequences of those old ties. He could live like a commoner and yet keep his royalty alive within, without losing anything. In Walid's view, it appeared, he considered himself the center of this particular world. And why not? He knew many people, and there were many women who wanted to sleep with him. He was wealthy, while the people he interacted with, many of them, struggled for survival. He considered Ron and me to be his closest friends, or the only ones he really respected, and I was certain he would keep that respect. We were older, had money, and had a good deal of life experiences. Young men respect this and often crave this kind of company. Most do not forget it. He sometimes also took the role of my protector. He would often save me from some annoying people by rudely sending them off, and when, he would see me talking to TP, would often express his displeasure after calling me to the side.

Alfredo was the one I felt most sorry for. I know I shouldn't have. It's not my place to judge or be patronizing. And I am certainly not being unctuous. If there ever was a wasted potential and life, his was it. He was a good-looking man of medium height and broad shoulders, one who exuded sophistication and intellect. He was very well-read and able to hold conversations on a wide range of topics. He was now forty, the father of two children. The two children lived with his ex-wife, close to his home. This way the children could grow up around both their father and their mother. Alfredo should have been a highly learned member of society. But at a young age, before he completed high school, he became a drug addict. For nearly two decades he struggled with addiction. It was during this time that he got married, had kids, and got a divorce. At some point, he dug up enough inner strength to control his addiction. Now he was mostly sober, but I am certain he would take something once in a while. I could figure it out by the way he behaved when he showed up those days. The alcohol and the drug, or drugs, running through him would push him over the edge. Those nights were ones when the bar had to make calls on his behalf to have someone pick him up. Fortunately, such days were few, and fortunately, he was never the garrulous, violent, loutish type. Even at his most vulnerable, he had a core of self-respect and great restraint. But mostly he showed up at the bar only to consume a few drinks to wind down. The years of drug abuse surprisingly did not leave any visible scars on him. Psychologically though, he carried the deep regret of missing the very early years of his elder son's life and was working hard to make up for that loss. He talked about his son whenever he could and never failed to mention how smart he was and how much potential he had. He would also mention in passing his greatest fear, that of his son going down the same destructive path he did. When I first started talking to him, he was working at a twenty-four-hour store, mostly handling the red-eye shift. He said he liked it that way. Those quiet hours, he said, gave him the opportunity to ponder, and work on the novel he was writing. He did not finish the novel during the time I was there. I know he started it, but I am not sure how big or small of a start it was. He was working on a fantasy novel, one with magical characters and such. He once went into great details and explained the plot and the characters to me. I could understand neither. I love fantasy as a movie genre, and I enjoy being visually led into a different world. Fantasy as a novel genre, however, never excited me. So, when he first talked about his book as we both drank, I tuned out. I felt somewhat guilty about it the next day, because I sensed that he was sincere in seeking my advice. But I later realized that he would have, either way, not completed the book anytime soon. I had once suggested that he write a novel describing his struggles with addiction. Perhaps, I suggested, he could write a book as a series of letters to his son, describing his life as an addict and what he did and experienced. It would be cathartic and would also make his son proud. It would certainly, I said, be more critically welcomed than the fantasy book he was saying he was working on. He never liked that idea.

Our first conversation happened because, while sitting next to me at the bar, he was excitedly explaining to someone seated on the other side the revolution underway in the field of biology.

"I can tell you, man, we're entering an era we've never come even close to before. We're not ready, man, I say, we're not," he said. "We cannot even begin to fathom. Just see how they're now designing life. I mean, they can literally design genes. They can break them, and they can combine them. They can do whatever they want. Whatever they want. They can do anything. They can tell these cells to fight diseases, or to become whatever they want them to become. Become dinosaurs too. Jurassic World is coming, man, it's coming. But you know what I am most excited about?"

"What?" the other person asked, rather indifferently.

"Think of it this way. We can design microbial life to withstand the extremities of Mars. Man, I tell you, if you pack up enough of those in a few rockets and send them and drop them strategically, we can cover the entire planet with them. And these microbes can make the planet livable for us."

This is when I jumped in. I am not one to let such an interesting discussion go to waste. "I think this is similar to something from a movie," I said. "I don't remember, *Mars*? *Mars*, was it?"

He turned towards me, and for a fraction of a second gave

me a penetrating look, perhaps trying to determine if I was worthy of being invited into his discussion.

"Yeah, I think I kind of remember. Or was it *Red Planet?*"

"Yes!" I exclaimed. "*Red Planet.* It was a good movie, I think. I don't remember much of it. Or any of it."

"It was okay. I remember it now, too," he said.

"Anyway," I continued, "sending bacteria to Mars is the easy part. They can do it now if they want. It's the radiation that's the problem. Mars has no real magnetic field. Its atmosphere's been stripped off because of it, and if there's anything living on the surface, it'll die quickly. Before they send those germs, they'll need to put magnets in its orbit to generate a magnetic field to protect it."

"Yeah, you're right," he said. "Man, I'll tell you, that's not difficult to do. They have the technology right now," and he tapped his index finger hard on the tabletop to emphasize his point, "right now, man, to do it. It's not even very difficult. All you need is solar power to generate electricity which'll create the magnetic field. You place a whole bunch of such satellites and place them strategically around Mars. And you don't even need to cover the entire planet at any time. All you need to do is cover the side that's facing the sun and deflect the radiation. You do it, and you can even have an atmosphere come back."

"So why don't they do it?" the guy sitting on the other side of him asked.

"It's all about the ownership," he replied. "There's this United Nations treaty done in the sixties or something on outer space. I think it says outer space belongs to no one and belongs to all. Now just think, if NASA or some rich billionaire makes Mars livable, which is not very difficult or expensive, but cannot take over it, then what's the point? Think 'bout it," he tapped his temple with his index finger to emphasize, "it's complicated, man, complicated."

Over the next year, Alfredo left his job at the convenience store because the hours were becoming hard on him. He joined a newly opened bakery in town where he baked custom cakes. I never tasted them, but I heard he was very good at his job. Baking cakes is a demanding job and the hours can be tough. He was the only cake baker at that place. The lady who owned the business was also struggling with running it, which was not surprising because it was her first business. One fine evening, unable to take the pressure and the owner's attitude, Alfredo quit and walked out of the place. He later joined a maintenance crew of a rundown apartment complex nearby. This was tough, hard work too, which strained his aging body. But it had a potential for growth. The maintenance crew was employed by a larger company in a big city. Alfredo saw himself moving and working there and getting a bigger salary. He was planning to get a certification or two on AC and heating unit repair.

For a while, for a few months, he was driven by one big goal. He wanted to go to New Zealand. He wanted to spend a few months there, work as farm help, and travel. He was first enamored, and then obsessed with, the idea of going to New Zealand. This happened because one day he overheard me talking about my trip to New Zealand and how I found the place to be very charming and idyllic. He started saving money for the trip, and he also filled out the form for a passport. He didn't care if it took him a while to save the bare minimum to land at Auckland. He was confident that once he landed there, things would somehow work out. He wanted to take his son with him and decided to save for two people. This way he could bond with his son in a way he had never been able to. Then, one fine day, he stopped talking about New Zealand. Completely. Not a word. I didn't broach the topic either. It's easier to give up on your dreams than work on them. It's even easier if your environment demands it. One should never judge a person by the surroundings.

The most enjoyable nights at the bar were almost always when Grant and Jack showed up. They were Jason's friends, and that's how I first met them. When together, we talked about everything, from sexual conquests and regrets, and women in the building on that day—topics never far away in a bar among drunk men—to politics, and to past personal history and future plans. Everything was kept lighthearted and nothing was taken seriously. It was an unwritten rule, one never broken. This was true even when discussing health of close family members. We were all there to enjoy our company. But there was something more, too. They were there because I needed them to be there. I just didn't realize it.

"It's never a dull day, gentlemen, when you're here," I said one late night to Grant and Jack and Jose, as I got up and started leaving the small round table around where we had spent a rumbustious hour.

"Thanks. We're here to help," Grant said.

"You know what we need here?" Jose chimed in.

"What?" I asked, knowing full well that a sexual innuendo was on the way. Jose was quick with these and had a seemingly bottomless reservoir. But this time he was quite drunk. Grant jumped in to occupy the small opening in the conversation as Jose was trying to collect his thoughts from his foggy mind.

"I'll tell you what we need. We need to bring score cards to score women here this Saturday," he said.

"That'll be something!" I replied with a small laugh. "I am sure we can get a few scores in before Ron asks us to cut it out or leave."

"Ha!" Jack shouted in his characteristically excited way. This involved leaning his heavy frame back, looking up at the ceiling, and making his round, bald face even rounder. Usually after this he would come back and say something in a hoarse, low-pitched voice. He was very rarely loud. "That would be something. All these older guys with score cards on this corner table. We'll even have a buzzer on the table whenever someone off the chart walks by. It'll be like those crappy game shows on TV."

"Yeah, but ours will be awesome, Jack. You gotta be positive.

Many of them will put up a good show if they know they're being ranked in a competition," Grant spoke.

"Gentlemen, you have dirty minds. Very dirty minds," Jose finally got something in. "I would not stand for something like this."

"No, Jose," Grant shot back, "we'll all be sitting for this, I assure you. It's the women who'll be standing and walking."

"Ha!" Jack leaned back again.

"I am so sorry you've been putting up with this the whole night," I said with a small laugh to Shelby, who had walked to the table to collect our bottles and glasses.

"Nah, you guys are just fine," she laughed back.

"Hey, are you going to be here tomorrow?" Grant asked me after Shelby had quickly collected everything from the table and wiped it clean.

"You know I will. What about you?" I replied.

"Yeah, we might. We are expecting a small consignment tomorrow and hosting a game night at the store. I might be a little late," Grant said and looked at Jack. Jack nodded in agreement.

"Why do you ask?" I looked at them.

"Oh, just wanted to know if you're going to be here in case we decide to show up. Hopefully it's going to be more crowded here tomorrow than today."

"I don't like big crowds," I said. "They give me panic attacks."

"I agree," Jose jumped in. "He cannot stand being around so many women. Perhaps he prefers only men? Men with hard bodies?"

"I like hard bodies!" I retorted. "Especially mine! I kill myself at the gym for it. Now I really need to leave and go to bed and wake up at a decent hour tomorrow morning. I like to pretend I'm a productive member of society in the mornings. I'll leave the two of you," and pointed to Grant and Jack, "to take care of Jose. He's dreaming of hard bodies."

"Ha!" Jack said as I turned and headed for the exit.

In a world that follows well-defined norms, Grant and Jack were anomalies. Jarring anomalies if one paid close attention. They came in seemingly from nowhere one fine day, after I had been a regular customer for two years. Grant and Jack were both interesting conversationalists in their own separate ways. A friend from work who met them when visiting the bar with me mentioned that their tall tales provided the perfect escape from the everyday. I do not think their tales were unbelievable. I do not think any story ever told is unbelievable. Grant, in particular, never looked like someone who sought validation in others' gasps and laughs. He projected an image of one who had fought many internal and external battles and won them all. In the process, he had gained knowledge and experience of many things, which he kept to himself and only hinted at if he felt like it. Both of them were in their mid-to-late-thirties. They were both heavy. Grant was tall, and Jack was short. Jack was clean shaven with a bald head, while Grant had a full set of long hair and a long beard. In their own separate ways, they looked like bikers, which in fact they were. Grant had been the president of a bikers' club sometime in his past. Both had been close friends for a long time. I do not believe Grant completed college. Jack once worked at the university as an adjunct professor in the Math department. He was considering looking for a full-time high-school teaching position. Grant was married to a former stripper who worked in a club where Grant was once a bouncer, and later became a joint-manager with Jack.

"A strip club for men is mostly quiet, but a strip club for women with male strippers is something totally else. It is loud, like really loud. Very loud," Grant once said. "Women go all crazy there and it gets difficult to control them. Once I had to be a male stripper. And this was when I was much younger and thinner, and much better looking than I am now. And I had a tough, tough time I can tell you. The women were out of control. It was all very demeaning. I cried when I came out. I literally cried."

I nodded. "Is it true that women strippers are all broken? Is that stereotype true?"

Grant looked at me, took a deep puff from his cigarette, blew out to the side, crushed his cigarette out, and looked back at me.

"Yes, they are all broken. In their own ways, they are all broken. And some of these strip club owners treat them really horribly on top of it. Like a piece of crap and a piece of meat. We two never did that. We would never do that. When Jack and I were running the club, we told them, I would tell them, 'Look, we know it's just a job for you and you're only trying to make a living. And so are we. Trust us, if someone tries to act like an asshole, you come to us and we'll take care of him.' And we did. I've had many fights outside the club, and some inside. I've had a gun pulled on me once."

"Really?" I asked.

"Really," Grant replied, and told me about the incident. Maybe he embellished it some.

Both Grant and Jack were gregarious types. They would always burst out laughing whenever I introduced them a particular way to my acquaintances, no matter how many times I did. I would introduce Grant as a gangbanger, but one I would enjoy being gangbanged by because of how his demeanor and physical attributes combined. Jack, I would introduce as a lovable serial killer, one who would make you laugh as he proceeded to stab you multiple times.

Grant was there the next night when I walked in. Jack had stayed back to close the store and would show up later. Jose wasn't there. He had to be at work early the next day. Jose was a shorter than average man, somewhat stout, who worked in a chemical company doing something I could never fully understand. He seemed to be someone who took his work seriously, and also simultaneously worked hard to take life on the lighter side. He would sometimes bring his work to the bar, too. He had an intellectual bent, one who appeared to have analyzed and examined many aspects of life very seriously. A bachelor in his early forties, he was never one to hold back his flirting, and sometimes passing outright very raunchy comments to women he regularly talked to. To them, he came across as harmless, fun company, one they could safely go to the bar with. He got along famously well with those who worked there, and I have reasons to believe that he liked them. At the very least, he did not seem to have any strong disliking for anyone in the bar or outside.

Conversations with Grant soon turned towards our individual exploits, past and present, and our failures.

"I am not just a failure," I said to Grant after I was sufficiently drunk. "I am pathetic. If I am offered sex on a golden platter, I would still not take it. I would pass the opportunity to others."

"That's so funny!" Grant exclaimed. "You would say, 'No. It's not for me. Take it. Take it away,'" and he followed on with a hand gesture, and we both laughed loudly.

"I would pass it to you, Grant, I would pass it to you. When a woman shows up at my door at one-thirty at night after she pulls away drunk from her own birthday party, and says she wants wild sex, what do I do? I take her to my balcony, have her drink some water, and then walk her back to her house party."

"Yeah, that's pathetic."

"Or once I left this bar at two at night, walked back to my apartment complex, and this woman who also lives there and was at the bar too but drove, pulls up her car and blocks my way to the complex gate, trying to pick me up. For those couple of minutes, she was persistent! She wouldn't clear the way until another car showed up behind her. But I did not get into the car."

"Did you two know each other?"

"No, I'd never seen her before."

"Was she attractive?"

"Yup."

"Yeah, then that's pathetic, too."

"Yeah, it is."

We both grinned.

"You know what's striking in both cases?"

"What?" he asked.

"What if the gender roles were reversed in those stories? What if I showed up drunk at a woman's apartment at one-thirty, or blocked the way for a woman walking home at two-thirty?"

"Yeah, your ass would be toast!" Grant shouted and laughed.

"And what if, just what if, I got picked up, and taken to her apartment, and then was unable to perform. Isn't that a scary thought too?"

"Nah! That's never happened to me. Such thoughts don't even cross my mind. I suppose you would get a reputation! Notoriety at the bar. Maybe even get hit on by women who would want to know if they are good enough to get you ready to do your job."

"The world is not for us decent heterosexual men, my friend, not for us," I laughed back.

"Aaaah," and he twisted his outstretched palm, "'sometimes-decent' heterosexual men. Not all the time. Sometimes." We both laughed again.

"You need to be trained!" Grant said after a moment of silence. "You need an education! I can do it. I have helped many, many nerds at the comic bookstore. We get all sorts of nerds. I have taken many, many of them under my wings. It's not for nothing, my experiences in life and my knowledge of comic books. You might be the most messed up nerd of them all, but I can still work on you."

"I am not particularly looking for a relationship," I said. "I just mentioned those incidences because you broached the topic."

"You'll be looking for something for sure. Everybody does. And when that time comes, you'll need help. I'll help you find that help. Trust me. I've never failed."

"What does that even mean?" I asked, thinking I had not heard him correctly over the somewhat loud music.

Our conversation was interrupted by the arrival of Jack. We had a few rounds of drinks and boisterous conversation.

"We need some music for what we're going to do next," Grant shouted over the loud music playing on the jukebox.

"Umm, I think this is called music." I smiled, pointing towards a speaker placed close to us, which was streaming borderline deafening music.

"Ha!" Jack said. "Not this music. Where's our singer? Did he show up today? It's karaoke night tonight, right?"

Jack had alluded to a struggling singer in his early fifties who frequented the bar. He sang multiple genres and could sing in two languages. He had many songs under his belt, some of them posted online. In all these years, he had been unable to hold a steady job. Ron gave him a few opportunities to sing at the bar. What he really wanted was to organize a small concert or, better yet, be part of a big one. He had once tried to get me to cover the cost of a concert, but had been rudely sent off by Walid. I did not give him any money for his concert, but did feel sorry for him, and continued to indulge him in small-talks.

"At some point, you need to come to some form of realization," I once told Ron as we watched him walk away.

"He's over fifty and he's still hoping he'll be picked up," Ron said. "There's a difference between childish dreams and childhood dreams."

"You know, Ron," I said.

"What?" He turned his face towards me and looked at me with wide open, very white eyes through his bifocal glasses.

"Success in a creative field is all about luck. It's got very little to do with talent," I said.

"I agree," he replied. "Listen to those half-ass worthless singers using auto tune."

"I'll tell you, I was at the Louvre a few years ago—"

"The what?" He cut me off.

"The Louvre. The famous museum in Paris."

"Oh, the Louvre. What about it?"

"I was there, and was walking around it, and came to the Mona Lisa. What a big crowd around it! It was something."

"I can see that."

"I'll tell you, it is a great painting. No doubt. But I saw so many there much, much better, by painters I've never heard of ever. Better by any stretch. But it's like everyone's decided that Mona Lisa is the best, the most famous, and no one can disagree. And it's not even that great compared to others. And there was hardly any crowd around the other paintings. The same thing, I think, happens with music, poetry, books, movies, whatever creative field there is."

"I agree," Ron replied. "It doesn't make sense, but that's how the world works. And they all carry their egos around pretending to be talented when they're just lucky."

"And so with this guy. I have no idea how good a singer he is, and I haven't heard his songs. I am willing to accept that he's good. If you've been singing forever with hundreds of songs under your belt, you've got to be at least half-decent. He should've had a steady job three decades ago and done his singing at the same time. He'd still have been a good singer. At least a singer who'd have been able to support himself. It's all about luck, Ron, it's all about luck. That's what success is. Someone very famous once told me something similar."

"And he was right," Ron had replied. "Must be a smart guy. We all think alike."

"Smart alright. A bit loony if you ask me. But smart. You're all alike!"

The singer happened to be at the bar this night, and when I ran into him, he was just a drink or two away from being very wasted.

"That's the perfect state I want him to be in," Grant said. "Hey, why don't you ask him to come by our table and sing for us?

"You kiddin' me?" I showed some exasperation. "I can't do that. He's been wanting to hit me up for some big money for a concert."

"Come on!" Jack exclaimed. "Let's do it. Call him."

I was tired, and so didn't argue. Why not, I thought. I'll give him some money and listen to his songs and figure out how good he is. I would still not support his concert in any way. I got off the high stool and went searching for him. After all this time, I still didn't know his name, and I wasn't very interested in finding out. I think he once mentioned it to me, probably the first time we met, and I must have promptly forgotten. I have a poor memory for names.

I finally found him in the patio, talking to a young man who was also inebriated, telling him about how the world of music worked. I patted his shoulder. His face lit up when he saw me.

"Hey, why don't you join me and Grant and Jack at the table?" I said.

"Sure! Absolutely!" He got up and followed me inside, leaving the young man to his drink.

Against my better judgment, which would have been far better had I not reached my drink limit, Grant made me buy the singer a very strong cocktail.

"Trust me," he had simply said. The singer had already crossed the line to be able to say no. We all watched him drown the drink in one big gulp.

"Maximo," Grant said. That's when I recalled his name. "Maximo, listen. Are you listening?"

"Yo."

"Listen. I want you to sing two songs for us. One in English and one in Spanish. Can you do that?"

"You know I can. You know I can do it. What kind of song? Here? What about this loud music?"

"Yes, here. And all this noise doesn't matter. We're helping our friend here."

"How are you helping me?" I had to ask.

"Ha!" Jack said. "We are. You just need to trust us and hear his songs."

"Give us a song to make someone soar high, up and above, to take wings, fly to his destination. You know what I mean, right?" Grant said.

"I know what you mean. I have just the right songs for you," Maximo replied. "You want one in English and one in Spanish? I have one that has both English and Spanish. How 'bout that?"

"That'll work." Grant made an OK gesture with his left hand as he deeply inhaled a cigarette with his right. "Just start when I tell you to, okay?"

"Okay."

"Here." Grant turned towards me, reached behind his back over his shoulder with his right hand and pulled out, from where, I don't know, a bunch of comic books and spread them around the table. "Pick one. Pick one that most catches your attention."

I looked down at the collection. They were all turned upside down. I reached out to turn one over to look at the cover.

"Uh-uh, can't do that." Grant reached out and placed his hand on the comic book.

"Then how am I supposed to figure out what I like?"

"You'll know. Ha!" Jack said. "Just pick one. And don't look at its cover."

"If you say so." I closed my eyes and pulled out a comic book and handed it to Grant. Grant took it from me and flipped through it before setting it aside. He quickly collected the rest of the comics and put them behind his back from where they had mysteriously appeared.

"Your song, Maximo. I hope it's good," he said.

"It'll be awesome, man, awesome. Once you hear the song," he looked at me, "you'll for sure help me with the concert. You'll be like, 'Man, I am really sorry for not helping Maximo sooner.' Yeah."

"Just do it!" Jack jumped in.

"Alright, alright, you guys are scaring me."

Grant stared at him. Maximo pulled out his phone and started scrolling through it. "Cool it. I need to have some music to go with the lyrics. I don't have my guitar with me, you can see that."

He hit on something and tapped it with his thumb. Music

began playing on his phone, and from what I could make out, sounded to be Tejano. It was difficult to say with the background din. His song was even more difficult to follow, and in just a few seconds, I gave up. Instead, I watched him and Grant and Jack.

Jack simply stared at Maximo with narrow eyes but an otherwise impassive face. Grant, on the other hand, opened the comic book I had selected and was deeply engrossed in turning and staring at its pages. Occasionally he would reach up to gently caress his beard across its entire length. In the nearly four minutes the song lasted, I did not understand a single stanza. I did notice that Grant's flipping of pages seemed to somewhat match the rhythm of the song. When it was done, Maximo crashed into the chair next to him, put his head on the table, and promptly went to sleep.

"Did you like the song?" Grant asked me.

"I liked it," I replied, just to advance the conversation to another topic. "He seems to be talented."

"Nah," Jack retorted. "He's not."

"Let me ask you," Grant looked at me, "and I want you to be very serious about it. Are you a tits man or an ass man?"

"That, indeed, is a serious question!" I laughed.

"Ha!" Jack joined in.

"No, seriously." Grant looked at me with serious, dark eyes.

"You know, I've never given it a serious thought."

"Come on!" Jack shouted uncharacteristically, with a brightly-lit face barely able to contain his laugh. "You can't lie."

"Okay," I said, and half-raised both hands. "Seriously! I've had no real preference as far back as I can remember. I just appreciate the female form. If I am in the mood for it, that is. I am getting old."

"Ha!" Jack retorted. "No man ever gets old. Come on! What's your preference?"

"No preference, seriously!" I replied. "I am living my life and enjoying it. Every person starts realizing the importance of life when sex stops being important."

"So, you stop and smell the flowers? Ha!" Jack said.

"Me, if you ask me," Grant laughed, "I don't do flowers. I do perfumes. Whenever the opportunity presents itself, I stop and smell the perfume. Okay, so you're telling me you're not into the figure as much as into the personality? Are you telling me you've never looked at those really short shorts, with half the butt hanging out? You're never like, 'let me follow it just in case it falls and needs me to put it back? I was heading south, but I'll follow northwest and then east and then southwest, wherever that butt's headed?'"

"It's not the destination that matters, it's the journey, Grant! It's the journey." Jack interjected.

We laughed.

"Alright, it's getting late and I need to head back home. It's been a tiring week, this whole week, and I've got a whole bunch of things to take care of over the weekend." With that, I got up. "I just don't know what you guys did here," I pointed to the lightly snoring form of Maximo, "but I'll find out from you next week if you show up."

"We'll be here." Grant looked up at me. "Here, take this."

He handed me his half-filled pack of cigarettes.

"Why would I need it?"

"That's your problem!" Grant retorted. "You don't trust. You need to trust."

"Trust what?" I asked, perplexed.

"Trust me," Grant said. "Him," he pointed to Jack, "don't trust him. Trust me."

"Ha!" Jack responded. "Don't trust me."

"I don't. You know that." I smiled.

"Ha!"

"No, take it. Think like you're doing me a favor," Grant said.

"How?"

"If I take it home with me, I'll finish it. If it's with you, it'll be fewer cigarettes I'll smoke. Just do it as a community service."

"I can do that." I smiled and picked up the pack. I put it in my pocket and left the place.

Chapter Five

the universe expands to lose itself

"Why are you still single?" I asked Orphia. We were sitting on the couch in my apartment and staring at a mindless game show on television. It was a very warm and sultry late afternoon.

"I don't know. Maybe I like it this way," she replied. "I've been busy with my work and never had time to think about these things. Why? You have problems with single women focused on their careers?"

"No. Of course not. You know me better than that," I said.

"I know, I know," she said, while still staring at the television. "I am tired of being asked this question. I know you don't have the intention, but everyone else does. I am tired of being an object of pity. I hate it when women are defined by relationships. And if I ever, ever make the mistake of letting my displeasure show, no matter how polite, I run the risk of being labeled an irascible old shrew."

"So, you still care?" I asked.

"Yes, I do. I do enough to avoid people and situations. I am not naïve. There are so many things in this world that are impossible for women to do if they are by themselves. The public space, sadly, is still owned by men, and women can run the risk of being treated as intruders to be harassed and driven away. And unattached women like me, you know, those beyond a certain age, are also looked at as outcasts. But I don't care for many of those things."

"We're not too different in our opinions, me and you, in this regard," I said. "But I am sorry if I said something unwarranted."

"No, I told you, with you, it's different. I think we had something together. If I were to spend my life with someone, I think it would have been you," she said matter-of-factly, still staring mindlessly at the screen.

"So, it's all in the past? Or is there a future?"

"Are you asking me to marry you? My answer wouldn't be a yes, you know that."

"I know. But it's not a no either."

"Just figure out your life first. Don't latch onto me to give you direction. I've been by myself and independent long enough and I do not intend to provide that service to anyone. Even you." She looked at me with not quite an emotive expression.

"Or an anchor?" I interjected.

She didn't say anything. We remained silent for a while, trying to absorb ourselves in the dull program. It wasn't easy. I finally gave up and went to the kitchen to make tea for us. When I came back a few minutes later with two cups, she had changed the channel to news. I handed Orphia her tea and sat down on the couch. We again sat silently for some time.

"Do you like children? Have you ever been around them?" she asked me.

"It's interesting that you should ask," I replied. "Have I ever told you about Shaun? No? I've thought about him on and off. I wonder where he is now. And I hope he's doing alright."

"Tell me about him." She turned around to look at me. She also lifted her feet off the floor and placed them under her as she leaned back into the couch.

"You want a story?" I smiled at her.

"Yes, I do." She smiled. "But not any story. I want your story."

I told her about my apartment and my neighbors.

After I had spent a few months out of prison, all mostly with no worthwhile human contact, I was ready to make a new beginning, to start afresh, and get back into society. When I first moved into the city to start my new job, I decided to move in with roommates, just like when I was in college or when I had taken my first job. I saw an advertisement online for a roommate, which mentioned a small, three-bedroom apartment with two rooms occupied by two men. The apartment conveniently also happened to be relatively close to my place of work. I called them up and learned that they were recent college graduates who worked long and odd hours. They were initially three friends in that apartment. The third friend had recently moved to another city with a new job, and they were looking for someone to replace him. They assured me they kept the place clean and did not appreciate loud noises. The rent here was relatively low, which was the prime attraction for them, given they were just starting on their professional lives and did not have a solid financial foundation.

In retrospect, I should have been a little sharper and more astute. The place was a stand-alone rectangular apartment building right by the intersection of two relatively busy roads. It had four apartments. Two at the bottom, of which I was in one, and two on the top. It was a rundown building, in a very rundown part of the town. I wanted company but wouldn't care much for it if it came at the cost of my safety. And I certainly didn't see the need to compromise on a half-decent standard of living I could easily afford on a fraction of the interest on my principal in the bank. But I had signed the documents for nine months. And so I stayed. I don't regret that I did.

In the beginning I never made any efforts to meet our new neighbors, and neither did they. Every evening, coming out of my car, I would see about five or six kids playing in front of our kitchen door. They would stop whatever activity they were doing whenever they saw me and would look at me intently until I passed by and entered my apartment. Then the din would start again. It wasn't irritating in any way at all, and I never bothered about it. Sometimes I would just open the kitchen door and watch them play while I prepared a meal for myself. Children are often compared with flowers, and that is not an accurate comparison. A flower may represent beauty, but it certainly does not, and possibly cannot, exude innocence. A spontaneous joy at seeing beautiful flowers is, on the other hand, innocence. Perhaps these two emotions have been often confused. Within a few weeks, I counted this group to consist of six members, five boys and one girl. None of them appeared more than eight or nine years old. In fact, the youngest was not older than three. Upon closer observation, I discovered that five of those kids stayed in the apartment that abutted ours. Another kid, a boy of about five years of age with the name Shaun, as I later found out, stayed in an apartment upstairs. On Saturdays and Sundays, when I would be in no particular hurry to do anything, I could see Shaun early in the morning ambling his way down the stairs, barely managing to hold his shorts in one hand and a plastic ball in the other, and would often give the appearance that he had not even bothered to wash his face. Upon reaching the adjacent kitchen door, he would bang it with his fists until someone opened it. Then he would ask 'Can I come in?' and he would be shown the way in. Thereafter, within a few minutes, the group of kids would again be out along with the commotion they carried.

Very soon, I started to observe our grown-up neighbors, too. Clearly conspicuous was a man in his early thirties living in the apartment with which we shared our kitchen portico: tall, well built with long hair and a face with striking sharp features, who would always appear to be lost somewhere up among the clouds, a classical portrayal of a Norse god. Whenever we met, we would acknowledge each other's presence with a nod but make no attempt at anything more. Staying in the same apartment was a woman who looked older than him by at least a few years. Her face was hard, as if she had seen and experienced the tribulations of life. Clearly the two were, going by looks alone, a mismatched couple, and in the beginning I thought these two to be siblings, later to find myself wrong. Staying upstairs was another man, around forty, average height with an aquiline nose. His eyelids gave the impression of being big, ripe fruits, ready to fall off at any time. Staying upstairs, too, was a married couple, slightly overweight. Both would return late at night and keep my roommates and me awake by walking across the floor of their apartment with heavy feet. They were struggling singers who worked at local venues. We never complained about their noise, which was just as well because they turned out to be nice people.

This was my neighborhood: six children, five adults, and, of course, those two guys that I shared the apartment with.

My initiation into this neighborhood-world as an active participant was with a threat to punch me on the nose. One evening, while I was standing in the kitchen portico with a cup of tea in one hand and my smartphone in the other, one boy came up to me and said, "Hey, Shaun says he's gonna punch you right on the nose."

I smiled and looked in the general direction he was pointing, where I saw a group of three boys and the lone girl. All four of them were looking fixedly at me, expecting something to happen.

"Where's Shaun," I asked, unable to make out who this young boxer was.

"Over there." The pointing finger moved frantically in the same direction, and its owner's eyes gleamed mischievously.

"Oh," was all I could say before Shaun removed himself from the group. Fearlessly, he walked towards me and said, "I am gonna punch you in the face and kick you."

The dialogues that followed are not important. I did get punched all right, but in my stomach, and I became a part of their lives. Perhaps to accept me, he had to hit me. Or maybe he had to hit me to show that he liked me. Or maybe none of it was true.

Children, children broke the ice, or, at least, the stalemate, between adults.

With those kids around me, conversation with the tall guy was now no longer limited to nonverbal signs. We would often stop and say hello or discuss the weather. It was around the time when winter had just started to probe the landscape, that we got down to exchanging our names and history. This happened during one evening when I was talking to those kids, while one of my roommates was in the kitchen.

"Hey man, what's up?" I turned around to discover the face behind the voice. It was that guy.

"Oh, nothing much," I replied. "And you?"

"Yeah, I am good, I am good," he replied back, and sipped on a can of beer. "So, are you working somewhere?" he asked after a few sips.

"Yeah," I replied. "I work as an engineer."

"That's good, that's good." He looked at me, trying to evaluate me more.

"It's okay, I guess," I said. "It's just a job. Pays my bills. Cannot complain."

"I get you, man, I get you." He pointed his fist towards me. After that, the conversation took its own course. He told me his name was Mark, and his wife, which is when I found out that she was his wife, was Laura. He identified his kids and told me their names. I tried hard to remember those five new names but soon forgot. The sixth kid was, of course, Shaun, who was the son of the guy upstairs, named Walt. For the next hour or so, I also discovered that Laura was an aspiring singer and Mark was her second husband. Mark had drinking problems in the past and would become disruptive at times. Laura was the only woman who, as he put it, understood him and helped him. Later on, I was to observe that this was perhaps not truthfully put. Laura, it seemed, was the only woman who could make him feel so guilty about his alcohol problem that he became indebted to her. She kept him to herself, not by love but by fury. He kept her to himself perhaps because she needed a strong man who could be easily controlled. In any case, he loved her and admired her and lamented his own insignificance. One day, he brought his wife and kids to our apartment. After a long eulogy, of which Laura was the focus, he asked her if he could bring her guitar and she could sing a few songs for us. She timorously accepted, but only after he allayed her doubts that we—my roommates and I—would not be disturbed, and would love it. So, she sang, and sang rather well. When we acknowledged her prowess, he asked her to sing another song, and another. Later when she was done, we got down to some informal, yet serious conversation. Mark told us about his wife, that she was a native American by origin, that her dad had somehow been involved in some kind of movement in the seventies, or at the very least had spoken against the government and thus paid with his life. Later this one-sided discussion devolved into government bashing, how it was trying to control everything, about the dangerous eventuality of everyone being fitted with tracking chips in their bodies, about the internet and impending doom, and the necessity to stock up homes when the going was still good. Then the discussion shifted to Walt and the fact he was a drug addict. This came as a surprise since he always looked like a nice guy, fully in control. His wife had died sometime back, and Shaun was the way he was, unruly and a brat, because of these problems. Then we were allowed into a piece of information that we all found quite ludicrous. The previous tenant of our apartment was, in Mark's words, "trash."

"He was something, man! Lots of problems with him. Had to be evicted by the landlady," he said.

So, here was an alcoholic, and then there was a drug addict, and the previous tenant was worse! Where had we come to?! Not a place for decent people to stay, certainly if those decent people could manage an accommodation somewhere else.

But we continued to stay. And I am glad we did. I became truly fond of these people, and they grew fond of me. Sometimes when Laura would drive Mark out of the apartment at night because of his drinking, I would give him something to eat. In the mornings, I would give him a pain reliever for his hangovers, and then listen to him lamenting on his addiction and the harassment his family had to face on his behalf. Shaun would also occasionally drop by. He would bang on our kitchen door even if it was open. Then he would ask, 'Can I come in?' and walk straight in. Sometimes he would catch one of us to give him a swing by getting us to lift him from below his shoulders and turning around in circles till we would get dizzy. After that, we would have to give a swing to the other kids too. Shaun's dad, Walt, would often stop over to talk to us and tell us about Shaun's latest escapades. It was quite a community, and very pleasing.

A few months later, Walt brought a woman to his house. Mark told me that she was a drug addict like him. I suppose birds of a feather really do have the habit of flocking together. Shaun, though still the love of Walt's life, was increasingly finding it difficult to come to terms with the divided attention at his home. When pushing away this new woman did not bring about the desired result, he came to us. He punched us and played with us. In the beginning, I did not mind him spending a lot of time with me. However, as the pressure of my work increased, I would sometimes find myself not only disturbed by his presence, but quite irritated. When my annoyance took a hold of me, it found a direction: Walt. I and my roommates would frequently tell Shaun that he should start going to school, and then we would drive him out of our apartment, with the hope he would badger Walt. The plan seemed to succeed when one day Walt told me that he was thinking of putting Shaun in school. This never happened as long as we were there, though. The only thing to happen was that Shaun became increasingly fascinated with the idea of going to school. He would construct stories of what he would do there. How he would tackle the bullies out there. What all he would learn. It was often very painful and sad to hear those tales: a child's desires taking wings, and yet being held hostage to an adult impotency, the impotency to take care of himself and his son.

Around the time when spring was planning on taking over this world, our world, things were not going well with our neighbors. One day the kids told me about the visit they had from the landlady that morning. Ostensibly they had not been able to pay their rent for a few months, and so were to be evicted within a week. I met Mark later in the evening and talked about this. He howled over the fact that he could not do anything for his family, that he had to find a job, and that he needed some small change from me to buy cigarettes. Hesitantly, I gave him some money, and they all left by the end of the week, leaving Shaun to play alone. Mornings he would spend by himself running around, evenings he would punch me for being late. When darkness would descend, I would tell him stories of monsters and goblins in the backyard to get him to go back home. I bought a few children's movies and picture books, so he could spend time alone. This plan backfired, though, because he would insist on coming to our apartment to watch those movies and have those storybooks read aloud to him

About a month later, Mark came to visit Walt and us. Sitting down with me, he informed me about their new home. Laura, it seemed, got a small break with some record company. Mark was going to join the police department and undergo extensive training. Walt was going to move out in less than a month because he was finding it difficult to get rid of the woman staying with him. Shaun's grandfather, as Mark told me, was a very rich farmer in another state, and he wanted them to stay with him. Well, I thought to myself, life has a way of taking care of itself. Things do sometimes work themselves out.

Shaun left, Walt left, and life became a little too peaceful for comfort. I missed the antics of the kid, his spontaneity and his sparkle, albeit a little overwhelming at times, but always exuding merriment and innocence. Nine months, five children. Five children who somehow, I felt, knew the truth about their reality but never allowed it to descend upon them, to take complete control of their lives. They all had the strength and fortitude, more so than those adults, to bear out their predicament with panache and without complaint. Or maybe I got it all wrong. Maybe they were just ignorant about life, and not, for their own good, mature enough to comprehend reality.

"Did you ever hear anything more about Shaun and the others?" Orphia asked.

"As a matter of fact, I did. A few months later, when I had left that apartment and moved to this one, I saw Mark walking at a local mall. We stopped and exchanged greetings. He avoided my questions about his police job but told me that he and Laura had separated and would, he was confident, get back together soon. He also told me that Walt had died a few weeks ago in a drug shootout and that Shaun was now staying with his grandfather on the farm."

"That's tragic," Orphia said as she ran a hand through her hair, looking at me.

"A big part of me was actually quite pleased over this news," I said, and took a final gulp of my almost cold tea. "Shaun was an intelligent boy and he needed a good home. I really hope he managed to find one, even if it meant the death of his father. Few people leave a lasting impression on one's mind, but Shaun most definitely did with me."

"I can see that," she said.

"I wonder where they all are now," I added. "This is not the first time I've thought of them. Perhaps it's because it's only relatively recent. We didn't talk for long in the mall because I had a few things to do and felt he found it embarrassing to present himself to me given his circumstances. We exchanged numbers. He hasn't called, and I don't think I saved his number."

"Wouldn't you want to meet Shaun and the other kids?"

"I don't know," I replied. "Maybe just to satisfy my curiosity. But I'm not sure. What if they're not doing well? What then? I don't really know how to help people. I never learned, and don't know if I want to learn now. I'd rather live with the illusion that everything's alright."

After I had come back from the bar the night Grant handed me his cigarette pack, I did something I had not done in ages. I pulled one out from the pack, opened a bottle of cold beer, and went out to my balcony. As I took a puff, looking at the empty swimming pool at this late hour, I heard a soft voice coming to me from my right.

"Hey."

I turned around to see a woman who looked to be in her early-to-mid-twenties, tall, with straight hair, at least in the limited light there was. She was in the balcony next to the one abutting mine, each separated by a gap not much over half a foot. There were four such balconies in a row, with mine being on a corner. Our balconies had their own featureless railings, which were short enough for one person to jump from one balcony to another with ease.

"Hi," I replied.

"I saw you at the bar tonight," she said.

"Oh, yeah, I was there tonight. Just like most nights," I replied and smiled. "I am quite a regular at that place. I don't remember seeing you there."

"I came out to the balcony hoping to see you. Do you have a cigarette to spare? I ran out of mine."

"Sure," I replied. "I have them inside. Let me get one for you."

"Thank you!" she exclaimed, but not too loudly. "I really need one."

I stuck my still-burning cigarette in a small gap between the railing and the wall. As I opened the door, I turned back to her.

"Do you want a beer, too?" I asked.

She gave it a thought for a very brief moment.

"No, I'll get my own. Thank you, though," she replied.

This was the only day she hesitated. She was careful about

accepting drinks from strangers. After that night, she would simply drop by and take one, or more, from my refrigerator. She would also bring expensive liquor once in a while, or call me to her apartment and ask me to down a shot or two with her. That didn't happen too often as I mostly avoid hard liquor. I also had very specific taste in beers. Nothing exotic or expensive. Since I drank regularly at the bar, I only drank lite beer, but of good quality.

I returned with the cigarette pack and sat down on the floor on the far corner and leaned back against the wall. She came out with a beer can. She then jumped over the railings to reach my balcony. That's when I had a much better view of her in the light from my apartment through the sliding glass door. She was tall and thin, and still in her early-to-mid-twenties. She exuded a cheerful persona, someone who would not mind breaking into a laugh at every given occasion. She sat next to me on the floor, took the cigarette from my hand, lit it, and took a deep puff, as someone who indeed needed it badly.

"Thank you," she said, the first words spoken in about five minutes.

"No problem," I replied and took a sip of my beer.

"I'm Anita." She reached out her hand. I shook it and gave her my name.

For the next three hours, until we were stupidly tired, too tired to even be drunk, too tired to even be able to stand up, too tired to even talk, we talked, and we drank, and she smoked, and we shared cigarettes. She brought me her collection of pencil sketches, which she pursued as a hobby. Many of them were very good. They were all still lifes and were bold with thick, deep pencil marks. They were clearly done with swiftness and confidence, suggesting that she was sure of what she wanted to do before she started. One sketch, I assumed, was a self-portrait of her topless below the neck. She quickly pulled it away from me when she realized I had seen it. Another one, of her closest friend, which she did not pull away from me, was her lying nude on her stomach on her bed. We talked about her fiancé and how they met. She complained how men would stop talking to her when they found out she was engaged. This led her to tell me we were sure to become great friends because we were very comfortable around each other and didn't feel pressured to look into each other's eyes. We spent a great while staring at the swimming pool as we talked. The undulations and ripples in the water caused by occasional gentle winds and the pool motor pump added to the quietude of the night and drove us deeper into conversation. It was when the sun had started to emerge that I called it a night. I don't quite know how she managed to jump back over those railings and enter her apartment. Despite my body being in a near-collapsed state because of extreme tiredness and drunkenness, I forced myself to stand there and watch her get in, just in case she had an accident. Then I went inside and crashed on my bed. When I woke up around midday, I did not remember much, other than just a handful of things we talked about in those three or more hours. I did feel that we had reached a tacit agreement to not sleep together, no matter what kind of conversations we had. I would not expect it from her, and she would not expect it from me. Or maybe that's what I made myself think.

We got along famously well, Anita and I. Her friends got to know me too, and I was led to believe—no, I was told— that I was almost always a topic of discussion when they met. Why? I don't know. What did they talk about when they talked about me? I don't know. Anita was a very smart woman. Book smart. Street smart. And smart about her makeup. She wouldn't think of leaving her apartment without it. She was on the showy side, and not far removed from bouts of histrionics. I had a strong feeling that she, on her own accord, would not amount to nearly as much in life as she dreamt of. But those flaws were added garnish to the sum total of her personality and beauty. Beauty is the blessing of youth, experience is the curse of old age. I do not know if time and experience would turn the entirety of all that into vainglory. It would not be surprising if they did.

I didn't see Grant or Jack that night, and for quite a few nights thereafter. When I met them finally about a week later, I had no idea what to say or ask. The entire matter from one point of view was preposterous and implausible.

"Hey, I am sorry I didn't bring your cigarette pack. It's all done. I'll buy you a new one," I said to Grant.

"Don't worry about it. I hope you enjoyed it." He didn't look at me but stared at the cigarette in his hand as he crushed it in an ashtray.

"I can't say I did. Or did not," I replied.

And this was the entirety of the conversation about that. I didn't buy him a pack, but I bought him a beer instead.

Anita did well to cover up any woes or hardships she faced. I knew there were challenges. She had talked about them. But she never dwelled upon them. She was, it seems, compelled to be cheery. We seemed to talk about everything and talk about nothing. We never went out together to a restaurant, breakfast, lunch, or dinner. Doing so would have taken our friendship to a new place. We went to the bar a couple of times together but nothing more. We would mostly meet late-nights.

"Can you recognize constellations?" I asked her one night around two-thirty as we walked towards the empty swimming pool, each with a beer in hand.

"No, I cannot," she replied. "Can you?"

"Not all of them," I said. "But a few."

I looked up as we each took a reclining chair in the pool area.

"Here." I pointed up and she brought her head close. Even at this late hour, she had her lipstick and perfume on.

"There, look at those three stars in a line," I said. "Imagine they are a belt. Look at the stars going down. Those are legs. And up there, do you see those two stars?"

"Yes." She followed my finger closely.

"Those are arms. And those the head. Do you see it? That's the Hunter's constellation. This, and the Ursa Minor, are really the only two so beautifully clear. At least these are among the easiest to see in city lights. If you can locate Ursa Minor, you can locate the North Star too."

"You seem to know a lot about stars." She looked at me with somewhat unusually wide eyes.

"Actually, and honestly, I don't." I smiled. "I am sometimes good at making things up. I have no idea if what I just said is correct or not."

"I think you should go into politics," she said after a brief silence. "I can totally see you doing it."

"And I can see you hosting some talk-show or game show on television," I replied. "You have the look and the personality. You should think about it."

She did not reply. We spent a minute or so looking up at the sky and sipping our beer.

"Do you ever think about what's up there?" She broke the silence.

I turned towards her and shrugged my shoulders.

"I am out of beer," I said. "I'll get one more and go to bed. You want one?"

"No. I have a long day tomorrow," she said. "But I'll join you, as long as you don't take too long to finish it."

We walked back to my apartment in silence. I opened a can and joined her on the couch.

"You never answered me," she said.

"Answer what?"

"About if you've ever thought of what's up there?"

"No, I haven't. I know there's something up there. There's got to be. It may not look big, but it's big."

"Do you ever want to go there and check it out for yourself? Suppose you could do it. Would you?"

"I don't know." I shrugged my shoulders. "I guess so. Or maybe not. I don't see the point of leaving all this behind and going into all that nothingness. But I am not saying I'm opposed to it. I am just not the wild pioneer adventurer type. What about you?" I turned towards her, only to find she had fallen asleep. I let her lie there. I used the silence to watch the TV and leisurely finish my drink. She continued to sleep as I went in to change and prepare for bed. When I came back to get a drink of water, she was still sleeping. I stopped to watch her sleeping form for awhile. Her mouth was slightly open, and she seemed to be dreaming about something vividly and frenziedly. Her eyes were moving rapidly, and her chest was heaving. Her facial expressions were also rapidly alternating between calmness and intentness. I considered putting a blanket on her and letting her sleep there for the night. But I couldn't see how this would be comfortable, especially since she'd mentioned a busy next day.

"Hey, Anita. Wake up. Time to go." I reached down and shook her shoulder.

"Um? What?"

"I said time to go. I need to sleep, and you need to sleep. I'll see you tomorrow." I stepped back as she sat up. She ran her hands over her cheeks and pulled her hair back.

"Do you want me to walk with you to your apartment?" I asked. She got up and stretched her back.

"No, I can go by myself," she replied.

"Great. Then just switch off the corridor light and close the door behind you."

I went to the bedroom and laid down on my bed. I heard her slam the door behind and I shut my eyes. But I couldn't sleep. Or maybe I was asleep and just dreaming about being restless. It must have been a dream. I heard the door open, but I did not get up. I heard the ruffle of soft feet as she entered my bedroom. It had to be her. We had shared keys in case one of us lost theirs. She bent over me. I opened my eyes and stared into hers. They were mesmerizing, enticing, glossy. Her perfume was intoxicating, invigorating. She broke into a broad smile and the whiteness of her teeth seemed to light up the dark room.

"I know you think of me as a comic book princess, entertaining but frivolous," she said as she gently combed her fingers through my hair.

"Or fantastic and illusionary," I wanted to say, but could not.

"You are illusionary for me, too." She seemed to have read my mind. "For all that I know, you may not even exist. Maybe I am dreaming all this. I find you very attractive, very different. But we're still here. We've defined the limits, which is expected from me. We've not defined the route, which should be your responsibility. We won't make love. You won't even try. You have these rules and I respect that. Your prison is not strong enough though. Not strong." She brought her face close to my ear and started whispering.

"You'll need to make it stronger. Much stronger. I'll help you. I am here to help you. I am a prisoner myself. All princesses are. They are prisoners. I know what it's like to be in a prison. You know it, too. You were in one, a physical one. It is stifling, regimented, choking. I know how to escape from prison. It's fun. It's motivating, it's exciting. The stronger the prison, the more worthwhile it is to break out. First, make your prison stronger, more insuperable. Then break it. I'll break mine, too. We'll liberate our prisoned psyches. I do not know what it will look like, or if it's going to be better. It'll be worthwhile. And then, together we'll make another prison. Bigger. Nicer. Fancier. Our liberated psyches will need another prison. We'll build them with our own hands and of our own volition. We'll not let them be built for us. We'll build them. Together."

It was still early morning when I woke up. Orphia had an arm tight over me. I tried to go back to sleep, but her hand across my chest was proving to be a hindrance. I delicately pushed it away so as not to disturb her and got out of bed. I took a while brushing my teeth as I watched myself in the bathroom mirror. My thinning, graying hairline caught my attention and I stuck the brush in my mouth so I could pull back my hair, hoping perhaps this would prompt my thinning hair to tell me what the future had in store for them. I kept the brush in my mouth as I looked into my eyes. I peered into my life thus far, as it played in my mind, from the earliest memories to last night. It wasn't bad at all, I concluded. Sure, there were regrets, huge ones. Sure, there were dreams and aspirations, bright ones. But it's one life. Of all the countless ways it could have unfolded, this was not bad. I put both hands on the sides of the sink and came closer to the mirror, trying to delve deeper into my mind. I had no doubt that I was a prisoner to it, to this life. But how long would it last? How long before the world crumbles the walls for me, leaving me exasperated, grasping for a straw to latch on to?

I finished brushing my teeth and walked into the kitchen. It took me a little longer than normal to wash the required utensils to prepare tea for myself. I did not want to make a commotion and awaken Orphia. Finishing up the remaining dishes could wait.

I made a particularly strong cup of tea. As an afterthought, as I looked at the steaming cup, I also added a small amount of instant coffee. This was going to be a robust concoction. I needed it. I took the cup and tiptoed towards the balcony. I kept the cup on a side table, and opened the sliding door gingerly with both hands, to make as little noise as possible. I did the same in closing the door.

It was a perfect early summer morning. The sky was clear, and the temperature had the right amount of crispness. The surrounding trees were agog with chirpings from so many birds, broken occasionally by the sounds of passing cars off in the distance. I sat on the floor of the balcony and stared at the swimming pool, sipping my tea.

"Hey!"

I turned around to see Anita standing on her balcony. She was wearing a strange combination of bright red pajama bottoms and a light green T-shirt. It dawned on me that this was the first time I had seen her in the early morning. She had glasses on and was without her usual layer of cosmetics. She looked no less attractive to me as she did with makeup.

"Hi," I replied, and stood up. "You're early today."

"So are you!" she replied.

"I woke up and couldn't go back to sleep," I said. She had jumped over the railings while balancing her cup of coffee.

"Oh, yeah? Lots of action? Must have been an overpowering feeling, getting laid after a while!" She broke into a sly smile and then bit her lower lip. "I am just kidding, you know that, right?"

"I know, I know, Anita." I smiled back. "I would never dare challenge you in the race to get laid."

"Ha!"

She looked at me, and for the briefest of moment I felt her digging into my eyes, moving rapidly, penetrating, exploring.

"I didn't see you two at the bar last night."

"No, we didn't make it there. We watched a late-night movie at the theater and decided to call it a night after that. Were you there?"

"Yeah. It was fun. You two should have been there."

"Oh yeah? What happened?" I asked.

"Nothing more than the usual weekend night, really. I ran into your friend from the comic bookstore, Grant."

"Oh, yes. How was he?"

"He was good. We had a nice time talking."

"Did he hit on you and try to take you back to his store?"

"Yes, he did!"

"And?"

"Stop being silly!" She took a sip from her cup as she looked at me. I did the same with my cup.

"He gave me a comic book to read. I told him I am not into them, but he said I'll like this one. I am going to read it when I get the time."

"Enjoy!" I said. "Listen, I need to get back in. She must have woken up by now and will soon be wondering where I've gone. By the way, what's the comic book about? Maybe you can give it to me after you've read it. It's been decades I think since I last read one."

"I don't know," she replied. "It seems to be about some princess or something. Take care!" She turned around to get back to her balcony.

I watched her enter her apartment and then I walked back in. This time I didn't bother to be quiet. I wanted Orphia to wake up. When I entered the bedroom, she was already out of the bed and in the bathroom. I went to the kitchen and cleaned up the remaining utensils and made a light breakfast. Soon she walked into the kitchen and gave me a hug.

We had our breakfast mostly in silence, watching the latest news on TV. We had the whole day in front of us with nothing particularly planned out. She had her flight out the next day. We decided to spend some time at the swimming pool.

The swimming pool was empty, except for a young woman with her toddler son, whom she was trying to teach swimming. We watched them sporadically, in between the leisurely laps we took. Soon we were joined by Anita. I introduced them.

"I saw you both enjoying the weather, and I just couldn't control myself. I have tons of work to do and know I'll regret this. But it's too good a day to miss out on some relaxation."

The two of them got along very well. Anita had no qualms about reaching across the age and experience gap with anyone. Orphia was always appreciative of any female company because she was in a heavily male-dominated industry. Most of her female friends outside work were also married and had different priorities.

I let the two of them do the bulk of the talking. I really had no big role to play there. It allowed me the time to get into the water in a far corner and remain there without being missed. I spread my arms and put them on the sides for support as I remained chest down immersed in the water. I looked at them again. They were still deeply immersed in conversation, seemingly oblivious to the surroundings. I wondered what they were talking about and thought of joining them. But I couldn't. I felt an overwhelming need to remain in that corner. If they were so engrossed it had to be something of some substance. Their facial expressions and hand gestures did not provide any inkling though. I pulled myself out of the pool and sat down on a pool chair. My thoughts were spinning, but none of them stayed at the forefront long enough for me to focus. I felt a strong need to push against something with both hands. I jumped back into the water and swam towards them with strong strokes.

"I am getting hungry. Do you want to get some lunch?" I asked Orphia as I raised my head above the pool.

"Sure," Orphia replied. "Let's go."

"Why don't you join us?" I asked Anita.

"I'd love to," Anita said. "I'll join you soon."

We went to a local restaurant and placed individual orders. During all this time, I mostly kept quiet, while the two women did the bulk of the talking. I again didn't pay much attention to their conversation. I was finding it difficult to concentrate on what they were talking about. Their voices at times seemed to merge into a single monotonous, low, rhythmic sound, and sometimes seemed to break into single-sourced multi-component sounds that competed for attention. Anita and Orphia could both be one single person for all that I cared. I didn't belong here, I realized. I had to do something to break this and break it fast. I had to do something to reach out.

"Let's go," I called out. "I think I am coming down with something."

They looked at me, and then looked past me, as if I didn't exist. They turned towards each other and continued their chat. I opened my mouth to call out to them again, but this time I couldn't even hear myself. Slowly, deliberately, I raised myself from the seat, to try to reach out to them, to touch them, to get their attention. I only managed to fall back on the floor. That's when I passed out.

"Shhh."

I could make out Anita's voice. But I couldn't see anything.

It was pitch dark. I was lying down on something soft. A bed, a pillow, and a blanket on top of me with just the right weight that I was used to. I was in my bed.

"Just try to relax and go back to sleep," she said softly. "You've been through a lot. You need your energy."

I promptly went back to sleep.

It must have been late in the day when I woke up again. Sunlight was filtering through gaps in the heavy curtains, brightening up the room. It was empty. I heard sounds coming from the direction of the kitchen. I raised myself up, first cautiously, thinking there was something wrong with me, and assuming this is what people in those situations do. Surprisingly I felt perfectly okay, even rejuvenated. I found myself wearing the same clothes I was wearing at the restaurant. I got up and walked slowly towards the kitchen. The sounds became louder. A strong smell of frying onions filled the air. It was Anita in the kitchen.

"You awake? Finally!" She beamed at me.

"Yes. But what happened? And how did I get back here?" I asked.

"You never left, in a manner of speaking," she replied without looking at me.

"What?"

"Don't worry. We have tons and tons of work to do. There's not much time."

"Time to do what?" I asked. She didn't answer but poured a cup of tea for me and handed me scrambled eggs on a plate.

I took the cup and plate from her and walked over to the table.

"I still don't understand. Weren't we at the pool and restaurant yesterday? Didn't I get sick and pass out? And where's Orphia?"

"Orphia is not here," she calmly replied. "Finish up your breakfast and get ready. We have to go."

"Go where?"

"You'll know."

"Know what?"

"Aren't you the curious kind! You have to go away from your old life. I'll help you. You know I am a princess, don't you?" She sat down in front of me, with her own cup and plate.

"I know. I know you are," I replied and took a mouthful of the egg, chewed on it a bit, and gulped it down with water. "There is no other explanation. Nothing else makes sense."

"No, it doesn't." She smiled. "Now we have work to do. We must break the walls. You must break the walls. It'll be tough work. I can help. I surely can. I have to prepare for what'll happen once you're out, too."

"How?"

"How what?" She picked up my empty plate and cup in front of me and stood up.

"How do I break the walls?" I watched her walk towards the kitchen. "And where's Orphia?"

"Oh, don't worry about Orphia!" She replied impatiently but politely. "We're not living in some long, bygone, ancient era. There are countless ways to get in touch with her. And no, trust me, she'll not feel offended if you don't call or text her right away. Besides, her essence is with me. Now, for breaking down the walls, that is a wholly different thing."

Anita came back from the kitchen and walked up to me. She stood beside me and put her hand on my shoulder. I looked up, into her eyes. She seemed to be towering over me, a larger-than-life figure. She had a glow that was at once calming and restorative, and stimulating.

"You don't worry," she said. "Don't. I'll lead you. That's my charge."

I turned my gaze away towards the balcony and stared at another clear blue-sky day. She did not move. I turned back towards her.

"So how do I do it?" I asked.

"First, you need to be clear about how you've led your life," she said.

"My life's been okay so far. No complaints," I quipped.

"I don't mean that. You need to have an idea of what's defined your life. Your guiding principles, if you may. Do you have any?"

"I am not sure I have any principles, so to say." I turned away from her and put my elbows on the table and clasped my hands.

"You don't? I thought everyone had *some* principles. At least, that's what people lead me to believe." She sounded perplexed.

"Nah," I retorted. "It's mostly what your courage and convenience permit. Those get passed off for principles."

We both remained silent for a few long seconds.

"I guess I try not to hurt others," I broke the silence. "Maybe that's my guiding principle. Though, I am not too sure. I suppose I would not physically harm someone if I can help it. I turned vegetarian because of it, you know."

"I know!" Anita let out a small laugh that surprisingly seemed to echo across the room. "That's a good start. Not wanting to hurt others."

We again stayed silent. I again broke it.

"Maybe I don't live by principles. Maybe I live by rules. I do have some rules, you know."

"Not habits? Are you sure?" she asked.

"No, no, not habits," I responded with surety. "Not habits."

"Rules it is, then," she replied, bringing excitement to her voice. She then turned around and walked away towards the balcony. She unlocked the sliding door and stepped out. I did not move from my chair. She came back a few minutes later and closed the sliding door.

"You could have used the main door, too, you know that, don't you?" I said, with a touch of sarcasm.

"I know, I know." She smiled. "It seems so much more natural and familiar to go that way."

She raised her T-shirt slightly to reveal what looked like a comic book tucked in her pajama bottoms. She patted it lightly to bring my attention to it. Then she pulled it out and placed it upside down on the table, slightly out of comfortable range for me. I did not make any efforts to reach out to it but continued staring at her for cues.

"Now," she said, "if you're going to move forward, you've got to leave the past behind. But you've got to also be very clear on what you're leaving behind. You've got to have a record of how you've lived your life so far. Exaggerate things if you must to concentrate on things you should. Minimize things if you must to disregard things you should. You say your life was largely defined by rules? Then you must define those rules. You must identify them. You must know them. Only then will we be able to break them. Only then will there be progress."

She sat down in front of me and opened the book to a random page. She did not look at the book. Instead, she watched me with piercing eyes, which made her penetrating gaze both commanding and demanding. It wasn't something you could refuse without being burnt. It wasn't a testy look, but the assured look of someone who's not used to taking no for an answer. It was unnerving.

I slowly got up from my chair. I then turned around and walked to my study, the second room in my apartment. I gently closed my door and began my task.

Chapter Six

the universe expands to escape its fiery core

"Hans," I said to myself.

"Hans. Why would he have the book? Why?"

"Hans."

"And he said Hans is at the dark end of the galaxy. What does he mean, 'the dark end of the galaxy?'"

I continued staring at the wall. Now that he had disappeared or dissolved, the wall, with all its jarring imperfections and sheer dullness, came into sharp focus. For a moment, I thought it was growing larger, trying to overwhelm me. I closed my eyes and opened them again. Getting up, I reached out to the glass and took a gulp of water. I walked out of the room and out of the apartment onto the balcony. It was dark outside. Unusually dark, given it was still evening. I stared at the empty pool and took a deep breath.

"Hey." I heard the familiar sound.

"Hi," I replied, without turning towards her. "Hans has the book. He's at the dark end of the galaxy."

"That's a problem, alright," she replied. I looked at her from the corner of my eye without turning towards her. She wasn't looking at me. She was gripping the railing with both hands, looking down towards the pool with me.

"Why him?" I asked.

"Only he can answer that, if he can," she said.

"And where's the dark end of the galaxy?" I turned towards her.

"It's at the dark end of the galaxy. Where else?" She turned to look at me. This time, she made no effort to jump over the railings to reach my balcony.

"How do we reach it?" I asked.

"How do *you* reach it. Not we. You. You've got to meet him," she replied. "But I can help."

"How?"

"I'll build a spaceship for you. I have her essence, I told you once, didn't I?" she said.

"Build a spaceship?"

"Build a spaceship. I am a princess. I can do it."

I looked at her to try to decipher what she meant. I could not. I turned around and walked back into my apartment without saying another word. A short while later there was a knock on my door. I opened it to find her outside, her hands clasped, with wide inviting eyes, but otherwise devoid of any expression. I moved aside to let her in. She walked in without any hesitation. I closed the door behind her and followed her to the kitchen. She walked over to the refrigerator and pulled out a chocolate bar. She broke it into two pieces, handed me one and promptly bit into hers.

"I'll build you the spaceship, I promise. But you'll have to journey by yourself. I cannot accompany you." She took another bite of the chocolate. I continued to hold my piece in my hand.

"So, what'll you do here when I am in the spaceship?" I asked.

"I'll wait. And I'll do whatever I usually do. Listen, I have to leave. I'll see you in two days. In two days exactly." She showed me two fingers for emphasis and then finished up the remaining chocolate. As she walked past me to head out, she handed me the wrapper and smiled. "Thank you!"

I went back to the bar that night after an unusually long time. It took awhile to greet everyone and explain my absence. This time I took my drink to a corner table. I had also carried a work folder inside. I opened it and pretended to work so I wouldn't be disturbed. I wasn't very successful. There was a regular stream of acquaintances dropping by to chat. I gave up and closed the folder and decided to focus on getting drunk. It wasn't long after that, or so it seemed, that Grant and Jack dropped by. They had brought their own pool sticks with them, ostensibly to play pool that night at the bar. They had both been serious semi-professional pool players in the past. Both had fancy top-of-the-line pool sticks and went to great lengths to take care of them. I watched as they played and drank and smoked. Eventually they tired themselves out and carefully unscrewed their pool sticks and placed them in their bags. Grant invited me to join them on the high stools. They would not have fit comfortably in the small bar couch I was sitting on. I ordered three beers, and when they arrived, I took them to join Grant and Jack.

"What's up? Doin' alright?" Grant asked. Jack was doing something on his phone. He raised an eyebrow towards me to acknowledge my presence and then went back to his phone.

"Doin' good," I replied. "What've you two good folks been up to?"

"Nothin' much, the usual," Grant replied.

"Any news from the comic bookstore?" I asked.

"No, same old, same old," Grant replied. "Thanks for the beer."

"Don't mention it," I said. "Hey, by the way, I am not sure, but I think I'll be taking a long trip. Hopefully not too long, but I am not sure yet."

"You sound depressed!" Grant retorted. "We'll still be here when you get back. When do you think that will be?"

"I don't know. Nothing's certain yet," I replied.

"Geeze, you sound like you're headed to the dark end of the galaxy," Jack jumped in.

"Oh, man, I don't know. Maybe." I turned to him.

"Ha!" he said.

"I don't know," I said. "You've met Anita, right?"

"Oh yeah, that hot chick. Yeah. She's a close friend of

yours? She talked about you. But you never told me you two are a thing or want to be one. I said to myself, 'why not?' and tried to interest her in coming to the comic bookstore after this bar closed," Grant practically bellowed.

"How did that go?" I smiled.

"Ha!" Jack rejoined.

"So, what 'bout her? Why did you mention her?" Grant asked.

"She says she's gonna help me go there," I replied.

"Where? The dark end of the galaxy? I can totally see her make that possible. But do you want to go? It's not fun, I can tell you that," Grant said as he lowered his voice.

"I don't know," I responded. "Should I?"

"It's up to you," Jack jumped in again after glancing away from whatever he was doing on his cell phone. "I would do it, if only for the novelty. I mean, how many times do you get to make that trip there anyway? So why not?"

"Yeah, why not," Grant chimed in. "Why not! Do it, I say, do it. And take her with you. And when you come back let us know how she is in bed. Don't spare us any details!"

"Ha!" Jack shouted. "Yah, give us all the details. Make it very embarrassing for us!"

"What're you getting worked up over? She's not even your type," Grant said to Jack. "He goes for the ones who are big," he looked at me and pointed to Jack. "Like big, as in big."

"Ha!" Jack responded.

Our conversation on this ended abruptly when Ron and Walid joined us. We had a few rounds of drinks and directionless merry chat. Near closing time, Grant leaned into me and whispered, "Drink up. Make sure you drink and drink a lot. Throw up and drink more after. Be sure to be super drunk when you go."

"Really?" I leaned towards him and whispered back.

"Really. Or you'll have a tough time. It's going to be tough. I had to do it once and I couldn't do it." He rolled his eyes and shook his head, which had the seeming effect of pulsating his beard. "Couldn't do it."

Before he could say anything further, he was interrupted by others who were pulling us into their conversation.

I drank more than my usual limit that night. I went back to my apartment and drank more. It was quiet on the balcony and I sat there for a while drinking, before going in and crashing in my bed. I woke up the next day and called in sick to work. I had a strong cup of coffee and a small breakfast and two ibuprofens with lots of water, and then went back to drinking alcohol. As evening fell, I considered going to the bar but decided against it. I was not in any condition to walk straight more than a few steps at a time. I drank more at home. A lot more. I threw up a few times, but each time I would follow it up with plenty of water, an hour or two of napping, and then more drinking. I do not remember when I passed out completely that night.

I was woken up by a combination of loud sounds cracking in my ears followed by sharp and strong shaking of my back. I forced my eyes to open. It was Anita.

"Wake up!" she shouted. "It's ready. You need to leave. Oh, you stink. Go take a shower and I'll get you some coffee and maybe some painkillers. Make it quick. You're late!"

I forced myself out of bed. I had to hold on to my pajama bottoms as I made my way to the bathroom. The effects of all that drinking had not worn off, not by any quantifiable margin, and I staggered all the way. I had to hold on to whatever support I could get my hands around in the shower. Showering helped. I came out feeling somewhat better than before. I got dressed in light, loose clothing and went to the dining table. I did not see Anita, but did find a cup of coffee and toasted bread on the table. I devoured these in no time and then slumped into the chair. Soon the front door opened, and Anita walked in.

"Feeling better?" she asked. "At least you look better."

"Yes, much better," I replied. "Thank you."

"Why did you drink so much?" She asked after a few seconds. "I've never known you to be this drunk."

"Grant ...," I started to reply.

"Oh," she interjected. "I guess he has a point. It's not a bad idea to be drunk when taking this journey. But not everyone needs to, you know. If you're strong, which you are, certainly more than him, you can handle it. But it can help. Come," she touched me on the shoulder, "let's go. Your spaceship is ready and waiting for you outside."

I was in no condition to question or argue. The effects of the coffee and the painkillers had just kicked in, and drowsiness, the good kind, the kind you know will relax you if you give in to it, was beginning to take over. I stood up from the chair. She reached out with her hand to hold mine. She then led me to the door and opened it.

Outside, just a few yards away from the main door, was indeed a big shiny spaceship.

The spaceship was huge. I had never seen one in real life before this, and the only comparison of size I had, as imperfect as it could get, was with what I had seen on TV or the movies. This ship was much bigger than what I could have imagined. The exterior was a glossy yellowish white, perhaps a bit too much. This imperfection, if it could be called one, was partially offset by a deep red paint on the fuselage, as well as on half the wings and vertical stabilizers.

"Do you like it?" Anita asked, looking at me intently.

"This is phenomenal," I replied. The wonderment of seeing the spaceship in front of my eyes made me briefly forget my physiological state. "It is very, very impressive. How? Did you make it by yourself? How did you get it?"

"Oh, don't worry about it. You just get in and take off."

"But, but how do I take off? I don't know how to fly these things. And where do I take off to?" I turned towards her fully.

"Don't worry again!" she exclaimed. "Trust me. I've taken care of those things. You'll find everything you need inside. There's also enough food and water. You just go in, push start, and sit back and relax."

"That's it? Are you sure?"

"Yes. That's it. Now go!" She let go of my hand.

I walked down the stairs and towards the spaceship. There was a small staircase that went up to the entrance of the ship. I climbed it and entered without looking back. When I was in, the door closed behind me automatically and the lights came on. The spaceship was very slick and glitzy on the inside, more so than the outside. It gave the appearance of a fancy upscale hotel lobby. I looked around and found the signs for the flight deck. I assumed I had to follow them, which I did. I was led through a few corridors and small rooms. Most of the rooms and nooks I passed by had furnishings and were very clean. Many walls were decorated with wall hangings and even tapestries. It was clear that the maker, or makers, of this spaceship were not unduly worried about expense. Indulgence was the norm for the maker.

"A princess alright," I said to myself loudly, partly to break the stillness.

I reached the flight deck, which had only one seat and a huge number of displays and switches. There appeared to be no windows, but the deck was well lit. The seat surprisingly, in contrast to everything else, appeared more functional than comfortable. I sat down and looked around. The large control board was intimidating. In front of me was a small lever with only two markings, Hans on the top, and Home at the bottom, which is where it was currently set. I looked around and behind me, expecting someone, anyone, to drop by and explain everything. But no one came. Finally it must have been the alcohol still rushing through my system, which reduced my anxiety and inhibition. I took hold of the lever, closed my eyes, and pushed it up. It was surprisingly effortless. I opened my eyes to find the lever in the new position. Nothing seemed to happen at first. Then the lights on the deck dimmed a little. I leaned back into the seat and gripped the handles. After that, things happened in relatively quick succession. The front wall of the deck slid towards the top to reveal a huge windowpane, corner-to-corner, top-to-bottom.

A strong vibration went through the ship following a low-pitch whirring sound. The sound died away, and the vibration also stopped. I felt a momentarily strong push into the seat as the spaceship took off. In the beginning, for a second or so, the lift was barely discernible, and then it increased. I did not feel anything, but saw everything outside and below on the ground grow smaller and smaller. The ship then stopped and hovered a great distance above ground. I could not overcome my curiosity and stood up from the seat and walked to the window. I saw the city and everything surrounding for hundreds of miles. I then heard a series of small soft chimes. In only a fraction of a second after the sounds ended, before I could even blink my eyes, the spaceship moved with unimaginable speed and was out of the atmosphere. It took me longer to get my bearings back. One moment I was looking at a bright blue sky above and around me and a huge landscape below, and the other moment I was out, with a bluish light emanating from the view below and a big bright yellow ball with an even brighter corona in front, and a dark background that seemed to overwhelm the view.

I was indeed in outer space.

The spaceship turned away from the sun and I saw the Earth below me in all its magnificence and glory, an intermix of thick cloud cover and clear views of the continents and oceans. The spaceship seemed to hover again for a short while. Then the series of chimes began again. This time, sensing another big event, I stepped backwards until I reached my seat and gripped the handles tight as I sat down. Just as the chiming stopped, there was another rapid movement across the windowpane in front of me, and the Earth was out of sight. I found myself surrounded by countless dots of light, big and small. I ran towards the window and tried to look around, but Earth was nowhere to be seen. It seemed the spaceship had traversed a great, great distance in space very quickly. However, there was no way of gauging that distance. Despite being surrounded by innumerable pinpoint lights, the only thing that struck me, which momentarily gave me a panic attack, was the sheer emptiness of it all. The loneliness, though, would hit me later. The darkness would become overbearing. I am sure I was moving through space. It would be ludicrous to think otherwise. But the distant background never seemed to change. It was the same. It was all sheer darkness. It might be bright on the inside, it might be comfortable beyond comparison on the inside, but it was an utterly miserable combination of darkness and emptiness on the outside. I fidgeted, I stomped, I ran, I jogged, I played with all the switches and knobs I could see. I slept, and slept some more. I ate just to pass time, even when I was overstuffed, sitting on my seat in the flight-deck and staring outside. I showered multiple times in short intervals, hoping each time I would be at my destination when I stepped out from the bathroom. I found a small bottle of strong liquor in a corner near the end of the spaceship. Underneath it was a short note signed by Anita.

"Just in case you need it. Perhaps it will help," the note read.

I finished the bottle in due time. I don't know how much time. I did not have my watch with me, and so had no inkling of the passage of time. But the alcohol helped somewhat. The darkness outside and the brightness inside seemed now to have merged into one single continuum. Both existed, both were real, both were consequential. I could not escape either one of them. I did not have to. Intuitively I understood why I needed to meet Hans beyond just the book. Intuitively too I felt I understood why Grant couldn't do it. This is no journey for one person to take alone even though it is only for one person to undertake alone. Only purposefulness can keep one on the journey if one decides to take it. My motivation must have been stronger than Grant's.

Once, after a generously long shower, when the effects of the alcohol left by Anita had worn off and I was considering undertaking another thorough search in case she had hidden more in other secret nooks, I heard the chiming again. I wasted no time and rushed to the deck. I did not sit down but went straight to the windowpane and tried to control my breathing lest my heart jumped out. It was beating very hard. Painfully hard. And soon enough, just when the chiming stopped, the view outside made another blink-of-an-eye transformation. No longer was I surrounded by stars. In front of the spaceship, almost close enough for me to reach out and touch, was a planet. I jumped with joy.

"Yes!" I yelled. And I jumped some more. "Finally!" And I leapt into my seat and held the handles tight. And then as soon as I blinked, I was on the surface of the planet.

The surface did not impress me. Truthfully, it was quite disappointing. For all the trillions of miles I think I must have traveled, I was expecting something exciting. On the contrary, I saw a mostly lifeless and featureless dry cracked and flat land with no vegetation within the view permitted by the windowpane. For a long while I stayed motionless, unable to decide on what to do. Part of me was hoping that something would drop in front of the spaceship, anything, and that would be my sign. But nothing happened. I finally gave up and stood up from the seat. If nothing else, this journey at the very least obligated me to step out of the spaceship, even if briefly, even if pointless.

With that decision in mind, I walked to the exit with alacrity. The door lock took a great effort to figure out. I would have given up, but I finally found the manual for operating the door. It was a single laminated page, in a small pocket in the sidewall. I followed the complicated steps listed and pushed the final lever with all the strength I could muster and quickly jumped back. With a loud whoosh the exit door pushed out and a strong draft of air pushed in almost knocking me off my feet. I walked to the door and stuck my head out. The staircase had deployed automatically. But what caught my attention was the landscape on the side opposite to the flight deck. The staircase reached down to a cemented pathway, which quite perplexingly ended exactly at the stairway. It was apparently a perfect landing. I climbed down the stairway and stepped on the pathway. Turning around, I saw it leading towards and up a small hillock not too far off. I assumed that the path had been laid out for me, and I took it. The walk wasn't unpleasant. The sun on this planet was bright, but it wasn't hot.

It became clear as I approached the top of the hillock that this part of the landscape was at the top edge of a deep gully. In just a few steps more the gully became a huge canyon. I found myself staring down a steep ragged canyon wall, perhaps a mile deep, or so it looked, with a river flowing at the very bottom. The pathway, however, did not end there. It took a downward turn, navigating the sides of the canyon. It was sometimes sharp and precipitous, and sometimes gentle, as it meandered towards the bottom. In places the pathway used natural protrusions of the canyon wall, but in many places it was clearly carved into the wall. Here and there, and in contrast to the barren landing point of the spaceship, interspersed along the path were ivy and other plants and small trees. Occasionally I had fleeting glances of small birds dashing around.

It must have been a good bit of time and walking when I reached the bottom, not too far from the river. I did not mind it. I had been trapped in the close confines of the spaceship for who knows how long. Days, weeks, or longer. I was enjoying this hiking immensely. The river appeared to be a flat-water river, fairly wide, and undoubtedly very inviting. But I still had the path to follow. It took me close to the riverbank, but slightly above the river level, perhaps as a measure against small floods. It then took a sharp turn away from the river and into a corner covered by a thick foliage, with the imposing walls of the canyon as the background. The foliage opened to a fairly wide circular grass lawn.

At the center of the lawn was a wooden hut.

The hut was not as small as the comparatively very large lawn made it out to be. The canyon wall juxtaposed on the background further reduced its apparent visual size. In actuality, it must have been at least a couple of thousand square-feet. And it seemed to have had a good amount of renovation and additions done on the outside. The pathway led straight to the door. On both sides of the pathway were regularly spaced small clearings in the grass, most likely done with the aim to plant something. The lawn otherwise was almost completely flat and covered with grass.

I walked up to the door and knocked, gently.

Nothing happened.

I knocked again, a little harder.

I heard a flurry of activity, of moving feet and clattering of something falling and being picked up. The movement of feet became louder, and the door opened.

It was Shaun. And behind him were the other five kids. And standing behind them was Hans.

"You can come in," Shaun said. "Where've you been?" He then playfully punched me on my stomach. I simply stood there, transfixed, looking at Hans. The children looked exactly as I had last seen them. There was no change. It had been some years since I last saw them, but they had not aged at all. Hans on the other hand, had aged, but aged well. He was as sharp as ever and was still standing erect with his chest out. He had an unemotional hint of a smile.

"Welcome," he said. "It's been a while."

"Hello Hans," I replied. "Indeed, it has." I was not looking at the children. I was hoping that if I ignored them, my mind would return to some semblance of normality. The long lonesome journey had clearly not been kind to my senses.

"You don't need to stand there." Hans's smile broadened, and the sparkle came back to his eyes. "He's inviting you in." He looked at Shaun.

"Oh, yes!" I smiled back and, this time, could not resist looking down towards Shaun and the other children. All of them were simply staring at my face with wide eyes. I stepped in as they made way for me. Hans turned around and walked into the passageway towards a bigger room, which I assumed was the living room. I followed him. He sat down on one of the only two heavy and elegant wooden chairs belonging to a small round wooden table. I took the chair opposite his. For over a minute we two simply remained in our respective places and did not say a single word. I looked around to take in the place. It was an unpretentious room, mostly empty and with bare walls. The table was on one end of the room, close to the small corridor connecting it with the kitchen. Another small corridor on a far corner led presumably to a bedroom, or possibly two. The ceiling, yes, I paid attention to the ceiling too, was fairly high and plastered. In all, the room appeared to be spacious, but nothing else.

As I took in my surroundings, the children also walked in and surrounded us. Shaun stood beside me. But the children remained quiet, pensive even. This was unlike my memories of them. Here they seemed to want to be mere, but avid, spectators to the doings of the adults.

Once the silence had run its course, I felt obligated to break it.

"Where is this place? Where are we?"

"I thought you knew," Hans replied. "This is the dark end of the galaxy. You must have traversed all that darkness and emptiness, dealt with the loneliness and gloominess and melancholia before you could get to this place."

"It wasn't a pleasant experience, I must say." I smiled. "But this place doesn't look very dark to me."

"It's because it's at the end of a journey. I am sorry!" He stood up with a jerk. "I am not being a good host. Let me get you something to eat and drink." He must have heard the low growling coming from my stomach.

He went inside the kitchen and I heard some commotion and a low decibel banging of pots and pans. I took the opportunity to talk to the children.

"So." I turned to Shaun. "How have you been?"

"Doin' alright," he replied. "Can you tell us a monster

story? Please?" He looked at me with wide, Bambi eyes. I couldn't help laughing.

"I think I've told you all the stories I know. No, really. I am not lying," I said, and looked at every one of them.

"One more, please. Please," Shaun said.

"Okay, I will. I promise. But not now. Let me try to remember some. Why don't you go outside and play?" I said.

"You promise?" Shaun replied.

"I promise." I put my hand on my chest.

"Yeah!" He jumped. "Let's go! Let's go outside."

He bolted out of the room. The others were not so enthused. They sauntered out, and I heard the door close soon after the last kid had left. The sounds from the kitchen had not subsided. It seemed that Hans was engaged in preparing something elaborate. This was just as well because the long walk had made me both hungry and thirsty. I had not realized this until now in my heightened state of curiosity and perplexity.

Hans came out of the kitchen in a short while. He placed a plate in front of me with a sumptuous looking sandwich. He walked back into the kitchen and brought two cups of coffee. He handed me one and took the other to this chair. We did not say anything until I had had a few big bites of the sandwich and a few satisfying loud slurps of the coffee from the cup.

"The kids have gone outside," I said. I couldn't think of anything else to say.

"Good," he replied nonchalantly. He did not make an effort to say anything more, and paid attention to drinking his coffee. I felt that he wanted me to carry the bulk of the conversation, at least at the beginning.

"Why are they here?" I asked.

"Who? The kids?" He raised his eyes towards me.

"Who else? Of course, the children," I replied.

"They are here so you can take them back," he replied, again monotonously.

"Now why would I do that?" I tried to sound a little irritated to elicit longer responses from him. I was not annoyed. I had no particular reason to be.

"You will because you have more reasons to than just the fear of making the back journey all by yourself." My attempt to change his disposition had obviously failed.

"I had not thought of my return journey," I said. "I've only just arrived." This time I smiled hoping a more positive approach might work. "I am not sure I am ready for it."

He said nothing but looked at me. I took this opportunity to finish up the remaining sandwich and the coffee. I made an attempt to collect the plate and cup and take them to the kitchen. Hans waived his hand. I took this as a sign from him for me to remain seated.

"Do you know why I am here?" I asked him, deciding to not beat around the bush any further.

"For the book?" He looked straight at me.

"For the book." I returned his look.

"Sure. It is done. I read it very carefully. Very, very carefully. It is indubitably a work of the highest order. No doubt. I have always been proud of you. I would not have expected anyone else I know to have been able to compose it," he replied. This time his expression changed.

"It was an effort alright," I said, and moved my head to emphasize my response.

"But do you know why it flew to me? Did you find out?" he asked.

"No." I squinted and frowned, hoping it would egg him on.

"Did you know that after we ran into our trouble," he said, which I felt was a very mild way of putting it, "I returned to your village and went back to the temple?"

"Yes," I replied. "I heard about it."

"I am old," he carried on. "I am old. I do not deny I am still burning with energy and still burning with the desire to live life. But all this has been tempered with realization of a very severe limitation. Perhaps as close to a fundamental limitation as one can get. No, it is not death. Death is not a limitation. It is an outcome of a limitation, another limitation. The limitation I am talking about is the mob."

"The what? What was that?" I asked.

"You heard it right. It's the mob." He put his cup on the table with some force to underscore his point.

"I don't understand," I said.

"I do," he almost whispered. "Let me tell you. I'll tell you. A mob is what you must fear the most. A mob is something that has no anchor, but has a big sail, which belongs to the wind. It will sail in whatever direction the wind takes it, to its victim. It has no moral or ethical bearing. It has no compassion and it has no desire for any empathy. It has only an identity, which is not the identity of its victim. I arrived at the temple with the hope to escape, what I now know and call, the minor mob. I hoped to spend time to channel my energy to rejuvenate and recharge and enter back into the world. On the contrary, I ended up spending a great deal of time meditating, being at one with my thoughts. I reached the furthest I could back into my memories. I analyzed them, understood them, categorized them, and put them in different silos. I toyed with them, ran multiple possible outcomes, and analyzed them, too. Hours and hours and days and days and months and months of meditation, of being one with my thoughts and nothing else. This was all that I did. I channeled all my energy into this. And each time I ran into that one limitation, that one limitation that circumscribed the limit of my imagination. I was lucky. I met the easy mob. Think of the more challenging mob. What if the mob comes to kill you? What will you do then? What if you are a parent with your family waiting for the inevitable as the mob approaches your house, your abode, your one safe place, or so you have led yourself to believe all along. What then?"

"What then?" I asked rather stupidly. This was after he became silent for a few moments and I could see him becoming darker.

"What then, then?" he retorted. "Imagine the wait as the

inevitable is bound to happen. You can't do anything. You look all around furtively. You can think of hiding, and you can think of hiding in creative ways, knowing full well the pointlessness of it. But you can hope. At the back of your mind is a hope, only a hope. No, not the hope of surviving. That's pointless too, really. It's the hope that this will be quick, that the suffering will be short. What else will you hope for? That you die before your children? That you don't have to see them suffer as they too meet the inevitable fate? That you don't have to hear their shrieks. What if, just what if, you are suffering at the same time as they are? What then? Will you be able to reach out to them? Will you be able to reach out to your son, to hold him one last time, touch him one last time, reassure him one last time that you are still his protector, as you and he have both been set on fire? What if your legs have been broken too? Will you crawl to him as you both burn? Will you hope he dies first, or you? What if it's not your son, but your daughter? What then?"

"Alright, stop." I raised my hand and almost shouted. "Stop."

"Or imagine ..."

"Stop!"

He stopped.

"I do not know what you're trying to get at," I said. "What's gotten into you?"

"The realization, the realization, that this is all, all that I have imagined, is not imagination. It is all within the realm of the completely possible, no matter where you are. The cruelty demanded by the mob can have no limitation, but the mob itself is the limit imposed on the individual. When I understood this, I had no further reasons to remain at the temple. I left. I came here. This is the only place I can be away from the mob. Nowhere else."

He again became silent. I did not interrupt his silence this time.

"Your book came to me. One morning, by the river, when

I was taking a walk. It flew to me. At first it looked like a bird. I realized what it was when it landed in front of me. It did not surprise me when I grasped what it was and who its creator was. I spent a lot of time with it, you know. I went through it with a fine comb. I looked at each and every rule you had written. I have never seen anything so comprehensive. It was at the end of the book that I also realized why it had come to me."

"Why?" I asked.

"Let's go out," he said, and stood up. I followed him out the door. The sun was still bright. The six children were busy playing, chasing each other around the lawn. Hans paid no attention to them. He looked up and whistled. I followed his gaze and looked up and around. Soon enough there it was, the book, swooping down towards us from a great height somewhere on the wall of the canyon. It flew with great speed but slowed down in front of us until it hovered in midair.

"Take it, it's yours," Hans said.

I reached out and grabbed it with both hands.

"Come, let's go back in," he said. I again followed him, back to my chair.

"The book flew away because it needed to be completed. I completed it. I summarized the knowledge I gained into it. Look at the last page. I have added three rules. Just three. These are the rules one needs to deal with the mob. Look at them," he said with some insistence.

I pushed my plate and cup aside and placed the book on the table. I touched the cover and ran my hand over it to reassure myself that it would not fly away this time, that I really had it in my control. I opened to the first page and read slowly. These were my rules, the ones I had written, the ones there to help me, the ones to help me break the walls. I turned the rest of the pages fairly rapidly. And then I reached the last page. There, not in my handwriting, were the rules by Hans. They were boldly written. Even the paper was indented. I quickly read the three rules. I then went back to the first rule he had written and considered it carefully. I then moved to the second rule and considered it carefully, too. I passed to the third rule and thoroughly reflected upon it. I closed the book and looked at him. He was staring at me, but his eyes were hazy. I stood up from my chair and walked out to take in the sun. The children paused their game and watched me carefully. Then in slow motion they resumed their play. I tried to clear my mind but found it difficult. I considered walking to the river and spending some time there. But I decided against it because I had a moment of denial concerning what I had read. Making up my mind, a few minutes later I came back and opened the book again to the last page. I read the rules again.

We two sat quietly for a long time, mostly still, perhaps thirty minutes, perhaps an hour. The only sounds were the faint, distant voices of the children.

When I had pondered over this enough, I said to Hans, "You are right. Your rules make sense. I do not see it any other way. It cannot be. Thank you for completing it. I can now go back, and go back in peace."

"And you." Hans smiled, and his face lit up just as I always remembered it. "And you. You no longer need to be bothered with thoughts of breaking any more walls."

"No, I do not," I said. "I do not indeed. I'll bid her goodbye."

"Yes."

We did not stay for long, I and the children. We had a hearty meal. I could not say whether it was lunch or an early dinner, because I had no way of knowing the local time. I did not bother to find out. Time seemed meaningless. While Hans was fixing the meal, I went out and called in the children. They were deeply engrossed in running around and at first did not show any inclination of stopping what they were doing. I called them again, a few times. They finally rushed in, quite excitedly, when I told them we needed to take the spaceship back home.

The meal was unexpectedly elaborate. I could not imagine how Han could have even managed to procure so many food items, let alone cook and prepare them. I thought of asking but decided against it. It was better to leave some things about Hans as mysteries. On any given day, people with lots and lots of money may face the same number of problems as people with very limited means, and they may be equally unhappy with their stations in life as the next person. But they have money. Lots and lots of it.

We spent the mealtime reminiscing about the past. We did not talk about the future. The only one to talk about plans for the future was Shaun. He talked at length about starting school and his elaborate plans for handling bullies there.

After the meal I once again offered to collect the plates, but Hans refused. He poured a strong cup of coffee for me and gave the children fruit juice. Soon thereafter I gave Hans a hug and we bid farewell. The six children followed me in single file, like a mother duck and ducklings. Hans stayed at the door until we were out of sight beyond the foliage.

The seven of us continued our slow walk towards the riverbank. We did not speak, which was just as well because for the first time I became concerned about the walk back up. It was one thing coming down, but going up would be more arduous. For me at least. For the little ones it would be impossible to complete in any reasonable amount of time. And we had nothing with us except for some light snacks and a couple of water bottles Hans gave us. For a fleeting moment I even had the thought of going back to Hans and restarting this walk better prepared. But I soldiered on. We would simply have to ration our supplies. And the hardship, if it could be called one, would be short. The spaceship was very well stocked.

The climb back up was fortunately not as difficult as I feared. The weather was pleasant even as we gained height, which helped. The path incline was mostly low except at a few places. The children were also in good spirits throughout. We stopped a few times but there were no complaints.

We reached the spaceship while the sun was still above the horizon. The dread of the impending journey was momentarily relegated to the back of my thoughts as the excitement of entering the spaceship and showing every interior part of it I knew to the children took over. We celebrated with hot chocolate. Soon some of the children, including Shaun, let out prolonged yawns. I took that as the cue. I wanted them to watch the takeoff before they fell asleep. Together, we all went into the flight deck. I asked them to move to the front, as I sat on the seat. Once we had taken our positions, I grabbed the lever and pulled it down to Home.

Epilogue

and two letters

In one sense, I told myself, we are all hurtling through empty space, each and every moment of our lives. This is the true form of reality, and oftentimes the entirety, of our existence. How does it matter if I am within the small confines of the spaceship or the small confines of my life back on Earth? Or what of the new confines Hans created for himself, for who knows how long? How are they any different? It is true that my journey to Hans was tough and lonely. But the return journey is much easier, relatively speaking. The comforting feeling that against all odds, with the calculations of probability overwhelmingly against me, I accomplished what I had set out to accomplish, makes this leg of the journey somewhat tolerable. I have the book. And I have enough time, more than enough, to spend with my book. I take it out from the small cabinet in my room whenever I can. After I am done admiring its cover, I read it, each and every page, each and every time I have it with me. Only now I know the proper way to read and appreciate it. I should have written it this way, too.

The return journey is also easier because I can imagine being back in the comforts of my home, the comforts of the company of the people I know, the sights and sounds I am deeply habituated to. It is also because the children are here. They give color to the spaceship. Outside it may be very cold and very empty. But inside, inside, is where it is bright, warm, and welcoming. I explored the spaceship once all by myself. Now I am exploring it again, with fresh pairs of eyes. I explored it once when I was inebriated. Now I am exploring it again, with eagerness and enthusiasm.

I have also used my time to compose two letters that needed to be composed—one to Anita, and the other to Orphia. Here is the letter to Anita:

Dear Anita,

It is with utmost affection and fondness that I am composing this letter. Your friendship has been of pivotal importance in my life, and I cannot be indebted enough. You helped make my journey as safe and comfortable as possible. I know many, perhaps most, are not afforded the luxury you made possible for me. I met Hans, and I have my book back. I am writing this letter because I do not believe I will be meeting you again, perhaps ever. I am very certain you may no longer be there. But I am sure this letter will reach you. It will.

You may already have an inkling of at least some of the conversations I had with Hans. I think I have found my own comfortable prison. I know the prison we two would have built together would have been the fanciest one possible—I know you! But this one is comfortable enough for me.

It may come as no surprise to you that the journey was tough. While traveling to Hans I was too self-absorbed to notice anything but the vast dark emptiness outside and the suffocating bright emptiness inside. On the return journey, though, I have had a chance to notice things in greater detail. Your ship is so awesome and so fast that I've overtaken a number of other ships making similar journeys back. I have, however, not seen any ship going in the opposite direction—towards the place I do not wish to go back to anytime soon, if at all. Maybe this is because those paths are different. It is difficult to say. Everything looks the same outside.

I have been reflecting a lot on what life will be when I get back and you are not around. I do not know if I'll go back to the bar again. Ron died while I was away. Who knows how it is being run now? Maybe I'll go back there for Grant and Jack and Chelsea and TP and Jason and others. The bar, I figured, has been more important to me than I realized, and may continue to be a powerful pull for me. I wish I had found that anchor sooner in my life. But the banyan tree in my village prevented me from recognizing it.

Did you emanate from that tree? Or from a comic book that Grant pulled out? I will never know. But you are gone, and Ron is gone. And Hans? Hans is as good as gone too. But he showed me how to face and overcome the biggest limitation. He showed me the rule for when to accept the limitation (mostly always) and the rule for when to reject it (mostly never).

I am curious about one thing, and it has to do with the design of this ship. I know you are not going to be around to satisfy my curiosity, but it doesn't prevent me from speculating. Of all the interior designs you could have come up with for the spaceship, why come up with such a dull, uninspiring décor? I am not complaining about the luxury. Not at all. But I would have imagined you to have taken great liberty with the interior. I know, I understand, you would never have made it in the form of the banyan tree near my village temple. But why not the bar? Why did you not design it like the bar? From one perspective, it would have made more sense. A flying bar! It would have been an apt metaphor for someone taking a trip to where you sent me. I think there was a deeper reason beyond just the ease of simplicity in the design of the spaceship as it currently is.

I am not one to debate whether the intrinsic value of a place is defined by one's company, or it exits on its own, in absolute sense. It certainly can be enhanced, and in many cases, made relevant, by the company. I can take in the beauty of a calm, perfectly blue sea on a clear day, sitting on the beach by myself. But I think it will be a different experience if I am with someone I enjoy being with. I can enjoy my balcony on a clear warm night alone. But it is just better with you. And after experiencing it with you, I cannot enjoy it by myself anymore. I will still sit on my balcony at nights, but the balcony and the nights will not be the same. In short, I think it is people that make a place.

In this case, in my journey, the bar by itself was not of paramount importance. It was the people in it, of it. And those people, for obvious reasons, could not accompany me on this journey. The empty bar, in fact, may have made the journey even tougher because I would have missed the associations more intensely. The association-free interior of the ship has certainly helped. I also feel I will not be able to travel in this ship anymore on such a journey because I will miss the presence of the children.

To the best I can do, this is my interpretation.

It is ironic that to break from a prison, to enter another prison, I had to travel in a prison. Our life is series of discrete prisons. We jump from one into another, and then another, and so on. I have experienced a few and I think I know which prison I want to be in. I want the banyan tree.

To Orphia I wrote a shorter letter this time. In it I expressed my love, and my desire to be with her. I also mentioned finding the book. I did not delve into the details of my adventure. This is because I will be meeting her soon in person, and there is a good possibility that I will not even post this letter to her. By the time I had finished writing the letter to her, and folded both letters and kept them carefully in my book, to eventually post them when I'll be back home, I had decided to leave my current job, my apartment, the bar, that life, and move in with Orphia if she will accept it, or somewhere close to her if she needs more time.

It is then that, I feel, my journey will end.

Acknowledgments

A big thanks to the entire team at Madville Publishing for all their hard work and dedication—Kimberly Davis for steadfastly being at the helm and never wavering in her support; Mike Hilbig for editing; Catherine Smith-Cox for the exceedingly beautiful layout; and Elizabeth Evans for proofreading with the finest comb imaginable.

A special thanks to Ashlee Rigsby for being the first to work with me on this book, just as with my previous two books. Her efforts have been invaluable.

Finally, thanks to my family for the immense support and patience.

About the Author

....

AMIT VERMA is a resident of Houston, TX, where he divides his time among things he is passionate about, including molding captive impressionable minds and conducting research as a professor in Electrical Engineering, a perfect family, and a never perfect yard. His two works of literary fiction, *The Lives and The Times* and *The Lives and The Times II* have been variously called a "rare find," a "page-turner," and "…Is refreshing and does a humorous take on some of the pressing Issues…"